November 2018

No Safe Home

Tara Lyons

To Cassandra,

Hope you're enjoying the DI Hamilton series - here we dig deeper...

With love,
Tara Lyons

Copyright © 2017 Tara Lyons

The right of Tara Lyons to be identified as the Author of the Work has been asserted by her in accordance Copyright, Designs and Patents Act 1988.

First published in 2016 by Bloodhound Books

Apart from any use permitted under UK copyright law, this publication may only be reproduced, stored, or transmitted, in any form, or by any means, with prior permission in writing of the publisher or, in the case of reprographic production, in accordance with the terms of licences issued by the Copyright Licensing Agency.

All characters in this publication are fictitious and any resemblance to real persons, living or dead, is purely coincidental.

www.bloodhoundbooks.com

ISBN: 978-0-9956926-6-4

For my mum – a real life Wonder Woman and a true inspiration

PROLOGUE

The creaky floorboards, at the entrance of her bedroom door, yanked her from sleep. If it wasn't such a regular occurrence, she'd have been annoyed by the rude awakening. Gone were the days of sleeping soundly; now she could hear a quiet sneeze from down the hallway, even with the doors closed. She supressed a small, internal grudge and forced her eyes open.

"Mummy, can I sleep in your bed tonight?" her son stuttered, more like a drunken person than a toddler.

She peered over his shoulder at the digital clock. The red, square numbers glared eleven forty-five p.m. – too early to give in to him, especially at his first attempt to crawl into her bed.

"No, sweetie. Come on, let's get you back to your room."

As much as she wanted to cuddle her five-year-old son, to pull him into bed with her and encourage some semblance of a good night's sleep, she knew it couldn't happen. Robotically, and in the vain hope of banishing the habit, she climbed out of bed, took his hand in hers and they stumbled together into the darkness. Their eyes half-open, they tread down the hall to the little boy's bedroom.

Thinking back to her childless nights when she would have stayed up until the early hours reading, or binge-watching an episode on Netflix, she groaned at the carefree time she had so readily taken for granted.

"But there's someone in my room, Mummy," he said, and stopped outside his bedroom door. "I heard something."

"It's just you and me, kiddo. You know that," she soothed, ruffling his soft hair. Gently, she edged him into the room. "Don't be scared of the dark. It's lovely sleepy time."

Prologue

"But why can't I have my night light on?" he moaned.

"I told you earlier, the bulb popped. I'll buy another one tomorrow. Now shh, into bed, sweetie, and no more talking."

She narrowed her eyes against the gloom, watching her son's shadowy figure finally hop back into his bed. Kneeling down beside him, she hummed a lullaby and stroked his soft cheek. The sound of his deep breathing quickly filled the room, and her own tiredness hit home like a hammer. Gingerly, she tiptoed out of his room, avoiding the creaks like a trained ninja.

Quietly pulling the bedroom door shut, she turned around and collided with a stocky, dark figure. A balaclava covered his face. She opened her mouth, but only a small squeak escaped. Her thumping heart urged her to move, to shout for help, to attack him, to do something. She considered scrambling back into her son's room and closing the door before the intruder made an advance. But stunned, she stood frozen in the dark hallway.

The stranger moved his head slowly from side to side; black eyes stared back at her from the two small holes in the thick material.

Her stomach clenched at the sound of his leather jacket crunching. Raising a gloved hand, he placed his index finger against his unseen lips. Thinking only of her son, she attempted to nod and pledge her silence, but her head barely moved. He snatched her arm, dragged her back to the main bedroom and slammed the door behind them.

In a blind panic, she scanned the room looking for something to grab, anything to use as a weapon, but could see nothing except her own tears. Fear gripped her again as the intruder spun her around, forcing their bodies within inches of each other. He panted loudly. His nicotine breath seeped through the balaclava and snaked up her nostrils.

He pushed her back onto the bed and took a knife from his back pocket. She closed her eyes to the sounds of a clink from the blade being lowered to the bedside table and a zip unfastening. He tugged her pyjama bottoms until her legs were fully exposed.

Prologue

She covered her face, grinding her palms into the sockets of her eyes. The bed dipped as he climbed on, and she felt his hot, wet penis glide intrusively along her naked thigh. She whimpered. But he continued to bring himself further up on top of her until his leathered fingers wrapped persuasively around her neck.

Just do what he wants, and then he'll leave.

The mantra repeated over and over again in her mind.

Just do what he wants, and then he'll leave; then my child will be safe…

CHAPTER ONE

Katy Royal spun around the bar pulling pints. Although she hadn't worked there for very long, she knew it was far too busy for a Friday night. The Tavern was a local, a 'regulars only' type of pub, where strangers barely ventured; it had been one of the factors which had attracted her to apply for the job. Her boss, Craig, had allowed a family in mourning to hold a wake there that evening and, although there were only thirty more people than usual, it was twenty-six too many for her.

Despite the sombre occasion, a couple of the men had made a move on her, attempting to flirt and buy her a drink. Thankfully, John, who had always sat at the end of the bar during the shifts Katy had worked over the past month, was quick to step in and save her. She hated the attention, and was grateful for his sympathetic nature, and his ability to swiftly move the drunken men away. It was John's salt and pepper hair and weather-beaten skin that made her guess he was in his late fifties. But for all that, he was a quiet man, uninterested in conversation, so she knew nothing about him, and didn't like to ask. Katy checked her watch, desperate for the last hour of her shift to hurry by. She despised working with people under the influence of alcohol, but it was the only job that suited her lifestyle.

"Will you work an extra hour tonight, Katy?" Craig called from across the bar.

Her boss shadowed her with his tall, athletic build. His sapphire blue eyes mesmerised her, and were complimented by the frame of greying hair on his head and face. Katy detected a Northern accent, but couldn't place its origin. She'd once asked where he was from, but Craig swore he'd been born and raised in Hertfordshire. And she had to admit, he definitely seemed to know everyone in the area.

"No. And you know better than to ask me that."

He marched towards her and bent down to her ear, whispering, "This lot are definitely going to want a lock-in. I'll sort you out some extra cash if you help."

She frowned, and looked him square in the eyes. "Craig, you know I have to be home by twelve-thirty, those were my conditions when I—"

"Okay, okay. I'm well aware of the conditions, but you can't blame a guy for trying."

He continued to serve the patrons, and Katy grabbed the metal bucket bin and left the bar to clear away the rubbish and collect empty glasses. The pub stood on the corner of a residential street, but there were a few tables outside, creating a makeshift smoking area. It was a quaint area and the neighbours never fussed, providing it was kept tidy and trouble-free.

Regardless of the crowd inside, Katy found herself alone outside, in the dark. She strolled between the tables emptying the ashtrays into the bucket. A hushed scream from the side alley caught her attention and she held her breath, straining to hear. Nothing. She lifted an empty pint glass and slowly walked in the direction of the noise, halting just before the entrance to the alley. A young woman twisted and turned under the force of a man, one of his hands covering her mouth and the other under her skirt.

"Get off her," Katy yelled.

He glared over his shoulder briefly, before roaring, "Piss off, bitch! This doesn't concern you."

"Neil! Neil, is that you? I'll tell your father if you don't leave that girl alone right now!"

The man released his hands and walked over towards Katy. The young woman took the opportunity to adjust her skirt and ran past them into the dark street, and out of sight. Katy edged backwards towards the tables.

"See what you done," Neil growled.

"When a woman is squirming under you, take it as a no."

"Or what, you'll run and tell my big, bad dad? As if he'd believe a bitch like you," he laughed, shoving his face into hers.

"No means no." Katy's voice remained determined, but she stepped back further again.

"For Christ's sake! What are you two doing out here?" Craig interrupted, his face peering around the pub door. "Katy, I need you back behind the bar, now!"

"I was just helping her with the glasses, dad," Neil replied, as he tugged the glass from Katy's hand and followed Craig back inside.

She exhaled a large puff of air and re-collected the metal bin bucket, her hands shaking, but not from the cold. When she entered the pub, Craig and Neil were nowhere to be seen, but thirsty punters all clambered for her attention. Swiftly, she jumped back into her role as The Tavern's best pint puller and got to work.

When Katy's shift was over, Pete was outside waiting. Her apartment was only a twenty-minute walk from the pub; a journey she was happy to take alone in such a quiet neighbourhood, but Craig had insisted from the outset he'd order a taxi when she finished the night shifts. New to the bar trade, Katy assumed the landlords of public houses would be bossy and selfish, but in reality, Craig was kind and considerate. The same taxi company was always used and Katy asked for the same driver. Thankfully, there hadn't yet been a night when Pete wasn't working. In her eyes, the fewer people who knew her address the better and, if she had to take a cab home every night, she preferred a driver who didn't want any chit-chat.

Within ten minutes, Katy was home. She climbed the stairs to her third-floor flat, paid Samantha for her time and flicked the kettle on. Samantha lived across the street and, although she was only eighteen, seemed more than happy to spend her nights babysitting. The young girl had done so most evenings since Katy started working in The Tavern just over a month before. She thought Samantha a very savvy girl; busy with college assignments and saving up to buy a car. It was more than Katy had been doing at that age, and she regretted not having been so focused when she was younger. However, it meant Samantha was a great fit for her, and therefore a great fit for Frankie.

Once alone, Katy peered into her son's bedroom and watched him lying peacefully for a few moments. His blonde hair was dishevelled on the Avengers pillowcase due to his fidgety way of sleeping. Regardless of his twitchiness, for a five-year-old, Frankie was a great sleeper. Every evening he was in bed between seven or eight p.m. and slept through the night until seven in the morning. His calming nature was a blessing to her. She crept in, tucked the blanket closer around his tiny frame and kissed him lightly on the head. Before leaving the room, she tugged on the window handles and readjusted the curtains so they sat flush together. Katy pulled the door, leaving it ajar, and then crossed the small hallway to the bathroom.

The reflection that greeted her was that of a stranger's. Make-up free, sunken cheeks and a wavy, blonde bob. She ran a hand through her hair and, not for the first time, wished for the return of her long, brunette locks and flawless complexion. Lifeless, blue eyes stared back at her. She quickly splashed cold water on her face, and vowed to spend more time on her appearance, just as she used to do.

Katy stepped back out into the hallway and twisted the key clockwise in the front door. Confident she had locked it straight after Samantha left, she continued turning it another three times regardless. She cursed the lack of internal wall space that prevented a chain guard being fitted, before finally sliding the double lock down and up again. It had become her routine.

In the kitchen, she peered out between the open blinds at the private garages below; there were six garages and a few disused cars parked in the bays in front of them. A small river ran behind, unseen, for the forest standing proudly in front, but the swish of water could be heard on a still night. The trees grew wild and ungoverned along the wooden fences and far into the private country common at the rear. Katy hated it. She didn't know who owned the garages, and people came and went at all times during the day and night to access them. The side entrance was a blind spot from her kitchen window and there was only one lamp post shining any light into the area. Tugging the handle to ensure the window was locked, she pulled the blinds closed and ran her fingers down them so they fell smartly into place. She removed an empty glass bottle from under the sink and carefully placed it against the back door. There was no need for the key to remain in this door because she had never used it. It led onto a small balcony she shared with her adjacent neighbour, and doubled up as a communal fire-escape back into the main building. The space had become a dwelling for unwanted footballs and furniture, overlooking the rusty vehicles below. The thought of engaging in small talk sent a shiver down Katy's spine, and therefore she never ventured out there.

Tiredness began to overtake Katy but she ignored it, choosing instead to make herself a milky cup of hot chocolate. As she entered her bedroom and switched on the lamp, she checked all the windows were closed and the cream curtains neatly met. Once she'd changed into a pair of jogging bottoms and a T-shirt, she slipped into bed. Smoothing the covers straight around her, Katy reached for her Kindle and sipped her warm drink, all the time carefully listening for anything out of place.

CHAPTER TWO

Sitting at a corner table of The Duke and Duchess public house, Denis and his team raised their glasses in the air.

"Sharon, it has been an honour working with you for the past couple of years," he said. "Our loss is most definitely the Vice Squad's gain."

"Can't believe you're actually leaving MIT for that lot," Lewis mocked.

Sharon jabbed him in the ribs. "Oi! Shut it, you. And thanks, boss, I've loved working with you all, but it's time for something new for me."

"Even better, when your replacement finally arrives, I won't be the new kid on the block anymore," Kerry beamed.

"Hey, you've contributed to some tough arrests in the past few months. You're certainly not the new girl now."

"Girl? Lewis, she's well into her thirties. Surely you can't call her that?" said Les, joining in with the banter.

"Excuse me! I'm not even thirty yet, can't you tell by my youthful looks," she said, framing her face with her hands.

Lewis and Les side-glanced each other and roared with laughter before draining their pints. Denis shook his head at their juvenile ways and retrieved the vibrating work phone from his inside pocket.

"You lot, excuse me for a moment." He made his way through the pub and out onto the cold street. "Detective Inspector Denis Hamilton," he quickly answered, before the call was directed to voicemail.

As his team were not officially on call, he frowned at the sound of Detective Chief Inspector Allen's rough tone barking orders into his ear. His stomach clenched as he absorbed the information, wishing he had sunk a few pints with the team and therefore be unfit for duty.

"I understand, sir. I'll be there in twenty."

With no time to gather his thoughts, and unprepared to face them right now either, he marched back into the pub. He scanned the table of drinks and realised his partner, Lewis Clarke, would not be joining him tonight. Apart from himself, Kerry was the only sergeant who hadn't indulged in an alcoholic beverage. Formalities dropped, Hamilton filled them in.

"Look, I'm sorry to have to ruin your farewell evening, but we're needed on a case. Fraser, you'll accompany me to the crime scene."

Morris waved her hand, dismissing the apology, while Fraser grabbed her coat and bag. Tolerance was key in this job; it wasn't the first time any of them had to leave a pub, family occasion or the comfort of their warm beds. They all understood, when a team is called in for a major investigation, it's time to make a move, no questions asked.

"Really, gov? I haven't had that much to drink," Clarke said, and folded his arms across his chest.

"A few pints are enough and you know that." Hamilton raised his eyebrows at his partner, who surrendered both hands in the air in agreement. "Fraser and I will handle it tonight, but I don't want to see a glimmer of a hangover from you, or you, Wedlock, in the morning."

The two men elevated their pint glasses – it wasn't the dutiful response Hamilton had been hoping for, but it was their night off. He left them to it, taking comfort in the fact they'd never let him down before.

The drive from Charing Cross to Kilburn was short and tranquil. Although Hamilton enjoyed Fraser's company, and she'd shown some impressive skills since joining his team four months ago, he was too lost in thought about the upcoming case to hold a conversation. A weeknight, and yet nightfall still enticed people to the area with its busy bars, restaurants and cinema. The streets of London never slept and Hamilton watched the strangers, oblivious to everything happening around them. Especially now, as Fraser navigated the route and finally turned onto a residential street, parking near the house they'd been called to; a home tucked away from the high street that had just become a murder scene.

Muted sirens blazed colour around the darkened streets, and neighbours stood on their doorsteps watching the activity unfold; some brazen enough to directly point their phones at the house and capture everything.

"Officer, get those people moved further away," Hamilton instructed, once he'd made his way to the front door. "If they won't get back into their homes, then they must get behind the barrier, now!"

His blood boiled at the invasion these vulnerable families were being subjected to, all in the name of getting videos and private information onto Facebook or YouTube first. They would be forced to watch their nightmare over and over, whenever it was shared, or liked, or tweeted again. A deep sadness consumed him; relieved social media wasn't as popular five years before. He knew only too well the evil power it possessed.

"Here you go, boss," Fraser interrupted his thoughts, and handed him a pair of shoe covers. "I just had a quick chat with that uniformed officer. The body's upstairs in the bedroom. Cause of death is unclear at this point, but forensics are doing a full sweep for prints and the parents are in the kitchen at the back of the house."

Hamilton lightly nodded. "Right… let's have a look up there first."

The muscles in his thighs were like cement, grinding and mechanical, forcing him to stop for a moment and abandon his ascent. Over twenty years of working for the Metropolitan Police had prepared him to walk into a crime scene and remain unemotional and detached. But, the brief details given by DCI Allen were enough to make even his hand shake as it traced its path up the banister.

Officials in white suits buzzed around the bedroom and the pathologist, who Hamilton had never met before, inspected the motionless body on the bed. He couldn't see the victim's face and took a few more steps inside, while Fraser shot off to speak to the attending officer.

Hamilton gasped and covered his mouth; he couldn't contain it. The young girl was wearing a Tinkerbell nightshirt, her long black hair fanned out on the bed and her glassy eyes bore into the ceiling, while vomit stained her chin. He looked away. Her laptop, on the computer table next to the bed, was open on her Facebook page and a sprinkling of white powder covered its surface. The pathologist stood up and outstretched her hand.

"Hi, I'm Audrey Gibson, one of the new head pathologists."

Hamilton tore his gaze from the screen and accepted her handshake. "DI Hamilton. I thought Laura might have been on call."

"She is, but on another case. Don't you find, as we creep towards the weekend, the crimes escalate like crazy?"

Audrey was obviously a talker, and right now Hamilton ached for Laura Joseph's military precision in delivering the forensic report. The new pathologist wore a warm smile, but he couldn't reciprocate the gesture, the thick air restricting any effort on his part to be courteous. She brushed the wisps of fiery red hair away from her face and peered up at Hamilton towering over her petite frame.

"Suspected overdose, Inspector." Audrey adopted a formal tone he was grateful for. "I'd rather not comment further until after the post-mortem. We'll be wrapped up shortly."

He offered a brief grin and swiftly left the room. In the hallway, Hamilton filled his lungs, drinking in the cool air as though he'd just surfaced from a river of dirty water. He bombed downstairs, the earlier cement in his legs now wobbled like jelly.

"Boss! Boss, are you okay?"

Fraser's puzzled face came into view, just as the weeping sounds echoed throughout the hallway and he nodded. Clearing his throat, Hamilton pulled himself up straight, recognising this was not the time to break down.

"Absolutely fine, Fraser. What did you find out? Because I've been told it's a suspected overdose, so I'm unsure as to why the first thought was to call us in?"

She hesitated, scanning his sweaty face. He remained quiet, scowling at her without a sound, and Fraser launched into an explanation.

"The victim is Paige Everett, a fifteen-year-old high school student. Found by her mother, Mrs Everett, who is adamant her daughter has been murdered, so we're here to scope out the initial crime scene. Are you sure you're alright, boss?"

"Let's have a chat with the parents." Hamilton dismissed Fraser's concerns, about-turned and entered the kitchen.

Once the formal introductions were made, Fraser set about making a warm drink for the two Everetts who sat huddled together at the dining table. The woman's auburn hair was pulled back in a clip, silent tears streaming down her pale face.

"My daughter did not commit suicide," she screeched. "She is a happy, beautiful teenager… she was…"

The woman wailed and her husband pulled her tighter to his large chest. Fraser placed two mugs of steaming coffee in front of them, but they were left unacknowledged.

"How could… not even be safe at home…?" Mrs Everett's voice was muffled.

"I'm sorry to have to do this now, but we have to gather all the information as soon as possible. What leads you to believe she was murdered?" Hamilton said.

Mr Everett's head snapped up. His red and swollen eyes tugged at Hamilton's heart. "Because we know our daughter, and she would not end her own life. I'm telling you, it was that boy who visited her earlier today."

"What boy?" Hamilton asked.

"I don't know, I've never seen him before. Paige didn't bring many friends home, and when she did, they were all girls. But, anyway, that's the thing, she wouldn't let him in. They spoke for a little while outside on the front porch, and then she stormed upstairs saying she didn't want any dinner. It was when my wife went to bed, to say goodnight, she…" Mr Everett lowered his head back onto his wife's shoulder.

"Can you tell us anything else about the boy?" Hamilton pushed for more details.

"Not really. I saw him briefly from the living room window. He was white. Tall. Older than Paige, maybe early twenties," Mr Everett mumbled.

"Okay, we'll ask the officers to have a chat with your neighbours and see if they saw him coming or going. Maybe he was driving a car," Hamilton said, as he stood up from the table. "We'll also have a chat to Paige's head teacher and her school friends. Hopefully they can identify this boy. I'll leave my card with you. Please feel free to call me day or night, if you think of anything else."

He knew they were no longer listening to him, but he went through the motions before leaving the house, hoping they'd be in contact with him soon. When someone takes their own life, especially a child, families automatically look to place the blame elsewhere, but Hamilton didn't want to discount the mysterious visitor.

As their car pulled away from the house, Fraser broke the silence. "That wasn't much of a description of the lad, hey, boss?"

"Fuck's sake, Kerry! They just found their daughter dead in her bed, what do you expect?" Hamilton snapped.

"Sorry… that was insensitive of me," she whispered.

He sighed, immediately regretting his outburst. "Look, it's late. Let's get home, have a few hours' sleep and regroup in the morning."

With silence restored, Hamilton's mind started to wander again; how was he going to tackle this case? He had changed so much in the past five years; having buried so much regret and torture, he wasn't prepared for the ghosts of his past to return to haunt him.

CHAPTER THREE

Frankie bulldozed into the room, yelling good morning as he jumped onto the bed. Katy opened her sleep-deprived eyes and hugged her son tightly. She checked her watch and chuckled. Seven a.m., he was like clockwork. Her fatigue was pushed aside just by the sight of him; the awkward way his blonde hair spiked up after a night's sleep, and the dimple on each cheek when he smiled. She was overwhelmed with the urge to protect him.

He settled himself under the duvet, switched the TV on and quickly became engrossed watching the Teenage Mutant Ninja Turtles, while Katy busied herself making them both tea and toast. After they had finished their breakfast in bed, and with the sun shining through the window, she relaxed on the pillow finally feeling content enough to sleep, knowing her son was safe beside her. With school on a summer break, and Frankie unable to enrol until the new academic year in September, this had become their morning routine.

"Where are we going today, Mummy?"

Katy pulled herself from the clutches of slumber and stroked her son's hair. "What would you like to do today?"

He hummed, tapping his finger on his chin, considering her question. She smiled, unsure of how a typical five-year-old would behave or speak, Frankie being the first child she'd ever really interacted with. He always seemed so intelligent and beyond his years.

"Can we go to the park, if you're not too tired?"

"I'm fine, and it's a lovely day. Brilliant idea."

"Maybe I can meet some friends to play with. You could talk to the other mummies and daddies."

"Perfect plan, sweetie."

Frankie turned his attention back to the cartoon and a pang of guilt stabbed Katy in the chest. When they moved from London three months ago, she had taken her son out of a nursery he'd adjusted to so well; she now worried it would have a huge impact on him. To then find out he'd have to wait even longer until he could join a local school, only intensified her anxieties. As always though, Frankie continued to surprise her as he swiftly fell into step with their new habits; some kids are resilient like that, she thought.

With the pair washed and dressed, they made their way downstairs. Katy was furious to find the main communal front door on the latch, open and unsafe, and not for the first time. There were eight apartments in the block of flats, leaving the unknown culprit to continually allow anyone to just wander through the building. She made a mental note to write another email of complaint to the owners of the building, once she had returned from the park.

"Frankie, come back! We're not going that way," she called out after her son.

"But, Mum! This is the way to the park. You said we could go to the park," he moaned.

"And we are, but we're going a different way today."

He scrunched up his little face. "But why? The park is just that way, behind those big houses. It's quicker and I want to get there now."

Katy closed her eyes for a few seconds; the need to frequently explain herself to him was frustrating, and sometimes she wished Frankie would simply listen without all the questions. Still, she had to remember his overtly inquisitive nature and, as clever as her son was, he was young and impatient and essentially, he just really wanted to get to the park.

She smiled. "Let's think of it as an adventure."

"Oh, you mean like a treasure hunt to find the park?" His eyes widened and he clapped his hands.

"Exactly! We've been to the park that way before. It's boring. Let's find a new way."

"You're so much fun, Mum! Okay, come on," he squealed, grabbing her hand and pulling her in the opposite direction to where they wanted to go.

New to the area, Katy wasn't entirely sure of where they were going. But the playground was surrounded by a huge swathe of grassland, and she'd seen people enter from all different directions on their last visit. She followed what she thought was the only logical direction that would lead them back around on themselves. Frankie skipped a few paces ahead of her, collecting large sticks and odd-shaped rocks, which he'd only abandon once the lure of the climbing frames and monkey swing came into view.

As they turned the corner, Katy wasn't the only one to spot the sign with 'Greenhill Park' written on it. Frankie shrieked in delight, shouting they'd found their treasure and quickened his pace from a skip to a clumsy jog. A man stepped out of the road adjacent to the park and blocked her son's path.

"Frankie!" she screamed, bolting after him. "Frankie, wait!"

He stopped yards from the man and turned around. "What?"

The air caught in Katy's throat as she caught up with her son and grabbed his arm. Her mind was clouded. She couldn't decide if she should whisk him into the park, hoping it would be filled with people, or run back to their home.

"Excuse me, do you know where Uphill Drive is?" the stranger asked, as he walked closer. "I feel like I've been walking around in circles for hours."

Katy shook her head repeatedly and pulled Frankie closer into her. The man frowned and curled his top lip. Her feet couldn't move and the silence was sickening.

Why won't he go away?

As if he read her mind, the stranger shrugged and breezed past them.

"Mum! Come on… can we go to the park now? It's just right there. We've found it!"

She mumbled incoherently, releasing Frankie from her grasp and followed him through the entrance. An elderly lady was crouched over collecting items that had fallen from her shopping bag, and Frankie stopped to help her.

"Oh, aren't you a lovely young boy," the lady said. "You've raised him with manners, dear. You don't see that type of behaviour very often these days. Good for you."

"Thank you." Katy smiled, and handed the lady a can of mushy peas.

Frankie ran into the playground and jumped straight into a game with a group of children. Katy held her breathe in anticipation. Occasionally, a crowd of kids were either related, or friends from school, and became cliquey, shunning a newbie to their territory. The first time it happened to Frankie, Katy was overcome with an alien feeling; she wanted to cry for her son, while simultaneously wanting to punch the spoilt brat who said he couldn't play with them. Deep down though, she knew that this was the harsh reality of life, and sadly something Frankie would have to learn on his own. He accepted it better than his overprotective mother, leaving the group instantly and amusing himself on the swings until a lonely girl entered the playground. He was drawn to her immediately, and they quickly sparked up a friendship for the next hour.

Katy was overjoyed to see it was a different troop of kids playing today and the young lad with the football threw it to Frankie. Her son had been welcomed. She looked over at the group of parents, sat chatting on a nearby bench, and smiled. That was enough to let them know she and her son were friendly, but she had no intention of approaching them or making conversation. Frankie wanted to make friends, and she was happy for him to do so, but it was the last thing she wanted for herself. Her son ran free, laughing with the other kids, while Katy dropped to the grass and sat alone.

After two hours of playing in the fresh air with a multitude of children, Frankie was finally tired enough to call it a day. This time, they took the quickest route home and Katy was horrified to find the apartment communal door had now been jammed open with the fire extinguisher from the wall. She contemplated creating a leaflet and posting it under every front door, but soon decided against it, afraid it would bring unwanted attention her way. For now, she locked the door with an exaggerated tut of annoyance.

Once inside, Frankie asked for a drink and headed straight for the sofa to get comfortable in front of the television. Katy knew he'd be asleep in a few moments, which worked for her; her exhausted body demanded some time-out. The blazing sun shone through the bedroom, but instead of opening the window, she turned on the fan and lay on top of her duvet. Something didn't feel right and she couldn't relax. Bolting upright, Katy stared around the room, a strange smell insulting her nostrils. She stood up and inspected the chest of drawers, which also homed her laptop, and then the dressing table. Her eyes roamed across the surface until she noticed it... her make-up bag was open and on the wrong side of the mirror. She shook her head, the tiredness causing her to leave things out of their usual place. Zipping the bag shut, she returned it to its usual position on the left-hand side. Katy now felt far too edgy to rest.

Powering up the laptop, Katy sat on her bed and composed an email, requesting management to remind all tenants in the building that the communal doors must be locked at all times. It wasn't something she enjoyed doing, it almost felt like snitching, but Frankie's safety was her top priority and she clicked the send button without another thought. Once Frankie had fallen asleep, she turned the television off and, as the flat fell silent, Katy peered over her shoulder, listening intently for a few minutes to check he hadn't woken up. Back in her bedroom, she selected the favourites tab on the internet taskbar, opened the Friends Online website and logged in to her profile.

Katy had only been a member for a month and hadn't uploaded a profile picture. Various people, both women and men, had contacted her and started conversations, and Katy was pleased for them. It was the only way she could make friends – if that's what you could call strangers on the internet. They didn't know what she looked like, who she really was and couldn't judge or hurt her. Choosing to be invisible, free to leave the chat rooms whenever it suited her, had a calming attractiveness to it. She finally had the chance to form thoughtful replies without speculation or command.

Butterflies fluttered inside her stomach as she bypassed the group chat rooms and opened her personal inbox. There was one message waiting, and Katy couldn't help beaming with excitement.

For two weeks now, private messages had been sent back and forth between her and Steven. They had a connection. Steven also didn't have a profile picture, but they had felt comfortable to share a description of themselves with one another. She had been honest, revealing her current appearance rather than the glamourous one from six months previously. The pair didn't skate into anything too personal, which appealed to Katy. As fond as she was of Steven, it was too early to open up her box of secrets.

A deep ache pierced her heart as she read the newest message from her only confidant. Steven suggested they meet in person. It was a subject they'd never discussed before, and Katy was disappointed he had broached it so soon. She didn't want to lose him as a friend and wondered how to let him down gently, not having dated, let alone flirted in over five years.

A noise from the stairwell outside the front door startled Katy, and she quickly pressed the power off button and shut the laptop lid. Tip-toeing from her room, she spied through the peep hole and her heart raced as two policemen strode past her line of vision. Her clammy hands rested on the cold wood, while she pressed her ear hard against the door. Inaudible chatter and muffled buzzing erupted from their radio transmissions, disturbing the once-quiet hallway. The sound of the policemen's uniformed boots pounding the stairs mingled with shrill screams. Deep voices echoed down from the flat above and crept under Katy's door. A baby's cry pierced through it all, vying for attention that didn't seem to be coming.

Leaning on the wall, Katy slid to the floor, wrapped her arms around her knees and sobbed. She stayed there for some time; immobile and listening to the comings and goings on the staircase, until her tears dried up. Her blocked nose and pounding head only added to the claustrophobic sensation that the walls were closing in around her. She sucked in a lungful of air, and exhaled slowly in a bid to soothe herself. It was the first time she had allowed the wretchedness to overwhelm her, and the first time in months since she'd cried uncontrollably. She hadn't been able to hold it back any longer and so, allowed the release to consume her.

Since moving into their new apartment, she had been strong, determined and focused on creating a safe home for Frankie. But, hearing the police stomp just inches away from her, caused her body to shake. Katy thought they had finally found her, that they had finally come to take her son away.

CHAPTER FOUR

Before Hamilton left to attend another murder scene, he rallied the team together in the incident room. Although they were only missing one member, it seemed quieter without Morris, and he wondered if he needed to request additional manpower while they waited for the new detective sergeant to join them.

"It's a nice split down the middle today," he explained. "Fraser and Wedlock, I want you to work on the possible murder case of the teenage victim. Let's see if we can get this one wrapped up as soon as possible."

"Shall we compare notes then, boss?" Fraser called out.

"What? Why would we need to do that?"

"Well... we attended the scene together and –"

"And you're a competent detective, Fraser. As we both saw and heard exactly the same information, what could I possibly add to this investigation?"

Although the room had been quiet before, Hamilton's outburst amplified the tension. With all eyes on him, he knew he'd unnerved them and decided to change his approach.

"Listen, someone is being transferred, but I don't know when Morris's desk will be filled. Yes, we have to work together, but I need to see some initiative from you all too. There's been another murder, a separate case that Clarke and I must attend. So, we have two fresh, open cases demanding our attention. Are you telling me this is too much for you?"

Hamilton had directed the question at Fraser. Her white cheeks flushed pink and she awkwardly tucked her long blonde hair behind her ears, but she looked him square in the eyes and shook her head in silent acceptance. He wanted to explain himself, but the right words wouldn't present themselves.

"Good," Hamilton said. "I don't need regular updates from either of you, I just want results. Clarke, our crime scene is in Pimlico and we're late. I'll drive."

The thirty-minute drive to Gatliff Road took them through Victoria Embankment and Parliament Square. Hamilton relished the journey through the busy city centre. He found the distractions captivating – the monumental sized buildings dwarfing them in history and fables and the cyclists whizzing by in their personal lanes. He knew the quickest way to travel through London was on the underground tube, but the close proximity of sweaty strangers would be an all-time professional low for him.

The radio played a familiar tune, and something deep inside tugged at Hamilton's heart. He switched it off and Clarke took the silence as an opportunity to divulge his recent love quest; he was the ultimate player and Hamilton hated it. However, feeling he had little choice, he allowed his partner to witter away, satisfied that at least Clarke wasn't speculating on his mood in the office.

Hamilton parked the car as close to the cordoned off area as possible and marched into the building, uniformed officers directing his path as he went. The apartment block looked more like a hospital than a safe haven to live in; the plain, bright white walls, the sharp angle of mirrored tiles in the lift, and corridor after corridor of identical front doors. A petite, black officer stood guard outside number twenty-six, but there was something about her expression that made Hamilton uneasy.

"Are you okay?" he asked.

She stood to attention, and although her body looked in control, her dark eyes welled with tears.

"I'm the attending officer, sir."

She tore her gaze from Hamilton and stared at the wall. He knew better than to engage her for further details right now.

It was a difficult time for a rookie – they always found it hard to shake away their first encounter with a dead body. When he first started working in the police force, he couldn't decide what was worse: a body found in a home, where people should feel safe and protected, or in a cold, abandoned hideaway void of love and compassion. He soon learnt it didn't matter, because discovering a crime scene was a horrific experience, regardless of its location.

"Stand down, officer. Go outside and get some fresh air," Hamilton instructed, and tapped her shoulder as a gesture of empathy.

He opened the front door and instantly flung his hand over his mouth and nose. A young lad from the forensic team, with a green tinge to his skin, was busy rubbing Vicks vapour rub under his nostrils. Acknowledging Hamilton, the pathologist handed him the tub and shoe covers from a nearby case.

"Christ! Couldn't they open the windows? I think my breakfast is about to make an unwelcome return," Clarke muttered, as he accepted the vapour rub.

"It takes less than two weeks for the putrefaction process to begin with the corpse. Gases that infiltrate the human body's tissues are released and organs deteriorate. They'll be scrubbing the smell of death from this home for some time."

Hamilton and Clarke exchanged stunned glances; it wasn't the reply either of them expected from the sickly-looking pathologist.

"How long has the body been here?" Hamilton frowned.

"You mean bodies... any time between two and four weeks, if the missing fingernails are anything to go by," he replied, and walked away down the hallway.

Clarke shuddered, fully covering his entire nose with heaps of vapour. Hamilton shot him a glance and rolled his eyes; after all these years, his partner still couldn't handle the smell. Audrey Gibson exited the master bedroom as Hamilton joined her in the doorway.

"Ah, Inspector, I'm afraid we meet again. Laura is having herself a well-deserved holiday."

"Audrey, hello. I must apologise for my behaviour the first time we met."

The small woman waved her hand in dismissal. "Nonsense! We both have difficult jobs and it's not like we can be upbeat all the time."

He smiled at the woman's genuine positivity and stepped around her to examine the scene. Hamilton's eyes began to water; not at the grotesque sight before him, but at the overpowering stench of rotting flesh. He coughed, suddenly wishing he'd been as liberal as Clarke with the Vicks.

The victim's bloated, black features and discoloured veins protruded through the skin making her unrecognisable. Like a naked starfish, the victim lay on the bed; her pyjama bottoms crumpled on the floor beside her. Hamilton backed out and followed Audrey into the large living room. A uniformed policewoman jumped up from her seat the moment he entered.

"Sir, I'm one of the attending officers," she quickly announced.

"I sent your partner downstairs. Tell me what you know and then you can get out of here too."

"The call was made by the landlady who'd had complaints about the smell. Also, the rent hadn't been paid last week and the occupant wasn't answering her calls. She used her own set of keys to enter the building downstairs, but said the front door to this apartment was unlocked. We've taken an initial statement from her, but she's more than willing to come down to the station."

"Okay. Do we have the victim's name yet?" Hamilton asked.

"Of course, yes… sorry, sir," the officer replied, and flipped through her notepad. "Scarlett Mitchell and her five-year-old son, Noah Mitchell."

Hamilton inwardly sighed at the mention of a small child, a fact he hadn't been made aware of previously. He jerked his head, signalling for the officer to leave, and turned to Audrey for further information; they were all parts of the puzzle to help him catch a killer.

"Inspector, we're ready for the bodies to be transported to the mortuary now. Please don't ask for cause of death; you've seen the body. I will need to conduct a thorough post-mortem. As for the child, I imagine he was suffocated… the pillow was still covering his face. Fear not, I will get back to you as soon as I possibly can. This scene is horrendous and I'll do my utmost to assist you."

"Thank you, Audrey. I appreciate that."

She purposefully marched from the room, and Hamilton overheard her shouting orders and delegating to her team. He wanted to know so much more about the bodies, but it became obvious Audrey wasn't the type to play ball until all the necessary forensic evidence was collated.

Hamilton tensely rubbed his temples, he knew his current mood was affecting how he interacted with his colleagues; both Audrey and Fraser had felt the brunt of his temper already. During his five years with the MIT, this was the first time he'd felt shaken by what he was facing. Although he had been involved in cases with vulnerable, abused and murdered children, they had never before come so close to his own nightmares. He worried his colleagues would uncover his secret.

He crossed the room and looked out of the floor-to-ceiling window at the spectacular view of the city; the tip of the London Eye illumined purple in the distance beyond the high-rise buildings. The River Thames glistened under the sun and the churning trains leaving Victoria Station screeched beneath him. He leaned against the window and caught his own reflection – bronzed skin without imperfection, an expertly short-trimmed black beard and closely shaven black hair – he was the epitome of strength and order. Inside however, he was breaking, emotions he had battled to suppress returned with a vengeance to haunt him. He pulled himself straight and made a decision: personally, justice hadn't been served, but he'd do everything in his power to ensure it would be for the little boy and his mother who had lived in this home.

CHAPTER FIVE

Five years ago

The pinks and whites of the floating cherry blossom petals fluttered in the warm April breeze. The entire day had been planned around when these trees would be in full bloom. The gentle wind, clear blue sky and delicate colours of the buds mingled perfectly. It was calming and beautiful and a symbol of hope for Katy and Brad's wedding day.

A new season, heavy with the scent of fresh beginnings, called to Katy like a beacon from the torrential sea that had become her life. Her world had changed in a fleeting moment when both her parents had died in a car accident, and yet here she stood two years later, being welcomed into a new family. The family who had saved her. She desperately wanted to close the door on the emptiness and despair behind her, and soak up every piece of delight Brad had to offer.

Their wedding day was spent in the exquisite Kew Gardens in London. Although they'd only known her six months, Brad's parents were overjoyed to see their son happy and spared no expense. Less than one hundred family members and friends joined together to witness Katy and Brad recite their vows in the flourishing private garden, and dance under a confetti of falling petals. The Cambridge Cottage, nestled in its own corner of Kew Gardens, brought everyone together for dinner and the evening reception. The chatter of guests, clinking of champagne glasses and applause during the speeches generated an electrifying buzz in the room.

While their guests enjoyed early-evening cocktails, the newly-weds slipped away and strolled along Kew Garden's Cherry Walk hand in hand. They began at the Rose Garden and followed the different collections of Japanese flowering cherries, stretching through to King William's Temple. As it culminated, with the pink blossoms soaring vividly against the white frame of Temperate House, Katy and Brad lit two lanterns in remembrance.

"I still can't believe how fast everything has moved between us." Katy wrapped her arms around Brad's muscular chest. "Do you think my parents –"

"Shh!" he interrupted, and pulled away slightly, just enough to force eye contact. "We've said our goodbyes to them now. You're moving forward with your new life. With us."

Katy couldn't disagree with him. Brad had already taught her the need to stop wallowing in self-pity and being selfish. She gently rubbed her small, protruding stomach and was once again filled with happiness for their future plans.

"You're right, Brad. I'm sorry. From today, it's about you, me and our baby."

He kissed her on the forehead. "Exactly! Now, let's get back into that party. I need a drink."

Once the pair had returned to their family and friends, the celebrations really began. The band kept the tempo high. Several shawls and ties were abandoned, dotted around the room over chairs and tables. Women disregarded their heels and danced barefoot, while the young men tried their luck with the single ladies. Brad stayed close to the bar, enjoying the free tab his father had arranged. Katy waved from the dance floor but he turned his back, evidently in deep conversation with someone she couldn't see through the crowd.

Suddenly, the two best men scurried around Katy, lifting her with ease into the air. Guests formed a circle around them, cheering them all on as her mother-in-law handed her a glass of champagne. She raised her glass in the direction of the bar, before allowing the bubbles to slip down her throat. It was the happiest day of her life. Katy never imagined she'd feel this immense happiness again and smiled at everyone around her.

By midnight, most of the guests had left. Brad's parents delighted them with one final surprise and handed the newly-weds keys to the honeymoon suite at The Richmond Hotel; a venue renowned for its views of the River Thames and Marble Hill Park. A car sat waiting for them out front, and Katy finally felt like the princess her father had always believed her to be. She had experienced the fairy-tale wedding she had always dreamed of having. She had hardly seen Brad since they released the lanterns earlier that evening; it was amazing just how much time was spent talking to people she'd never met before. Katy craved to be alone with her new husband.

Once the porter had shown them to their suite, they waited in the corridor for him to leave. Katy couldn't quite believe that after everything she'd faced, the man of her dreams was about to carry her over the threshold. Her heart sank when Brad opened the door, waltzed inside and made a beeline for the complimentary bottle of champagne. She quickly stepped in behind him, closed the door and ran her hand over Brad's back.

"Babe, is everything okay?"

He spun around and forced her onto the bed. Jumping on top, he straddled her and gripped her face. The tears sprung from her eyes, while his fingers pinched her cheeks so hard she was rendered speechless.

"You think it's okay to sexy dance with *my* friends? Did you honestly think I wouldn't see you? And drinking alcohol when you're pregnant. That's my child in there, so don't you ever endanger its life again. What kind of a mother are you?" he hissed, pointing at her stomach.

The reality of his drunkenness hit her and, never having seen Brad's temper before, Katy whimpered underneath him.

"I ever see that kind of behaviour from you again, and you'll be sorry. You're my wife now, act like it and don't fucking disrespect me. Do you understand?"

She mumbled, nodding her head as a fresh, wet stream of tears dripped into her ears.

"Good. Now take that blasted dress off."

Brad clambered off her and drank the champagne straight from the bottle. Katy fumbled with the zip on the side of her lace gown, oblivious to how her perfect day was transforming into the beginning of her nightmare.

CHAPTER SIX

Moonlight slithered through Katy's open curtains, a small offering of light in her darkening bedroom. Frankie had been asleep for two hours and she'd already washed the dishes, scrubbed the kitchen and cleaned his toys away. The idea of soaking in a hot bath was an enticing thought, but she was confident that even a relaxing time-out wouldn't work for her; there was no pleasure in unwinding.

Katy reached over to the bedside table and opened the drawer, lifting out her old black iPhone. She twisted it in her hands, wiped the screen clean and finally switched the power button on. While the mobile's apps and information loaded, Katy's heart pounded inside her chest. It wasn't the first time she'd turned it on in the last three months, but it always had this effect on her. Other than Frankie, it was the only link to her past she had brought with her.

She opened the photos app and pored longingly over the photographs dating back to her son's third birthday. Slowly, she thumbed between them, some holding her attention longer than others; Brad's smiling face during their family Christmas dinner just eight months before was a harsh reminder of how drastically her life had changed. Katy stared at her husband's face – his turquoise eyes, his blonde, curly hair and his chiselled jawline. He had been everything she'd needed, a saviour pulling her from the depths of misery, and when she'd been alone and scared, he had scooped her up into his life. Looking back, she often wondered if she'd imagined their wedding day, sordid and frightening as it was. A whole year had passed, then Frankie was born and they'd moved into a two-bedroom maisonette in Covent Garden. Katy had begun to depend on others again; her new family and friends became a comforting crutch in a life she'd forgotten existed.

Katy skimmed back through the folder to photos of another memory. Frankie's birthday, a bittersweet date, and she threw the phone down onto the bed. Hot tears burned tracks down her cheeks when she thought of the pleasure Brad had stolen from that day. On what should have been a joyous occasion, Katy had been humiliated; slapped in the face in front of their guests, a form of punishment no one stopped, argued against, or comforted her. It was all quickly glossed over and never mentioned again.

Thinking back, Katy recognised Brad's fury was unmasked whenever she enjoyed herself. She jumped off the bed and paced the room, fears and uncertainties scrambled through her mind. Switching the power off, Katy chucked the phone back to its hiding place and slammed the drawer shut. But, it did nothing to shield the thoughts of her last encounter with Brad; those terrifying images of trickling blood and sounds of helpless cries.

A knock at the front door dragged Katy from her haunted memories. She didn't need to check the time; it was far too late for the postman and he was the only one who ever knocked.

"Hello." A voice from the other side of the door broke the silence again. "It's me, Alexina. Your neighbour from upstairs."

"It's me, she says. Like we're friends," Katy whispered to herself, edging closer to the hallway and holding her breath to listen.

With any luck the woman's given up and returned home.

"Don't leave me standing out here, I'm in my pyjamas." Alexina's pitch increased and the giggle echoed around the hall.

Worried her neighbour would wake Frankie, Katy twisted the keys and, opening the door to a mere crack, peered out.

"Yes, can I help you?" she asked impatiently.

"Oh, hi! I didn't think you were going to answer."

Alexina stood unabashed in a silk camisole and matching trousers, holding a bottle of white wine. Her shiny, black hair fell poker-straight to her shoulders, and her chocolate eyes shone from the warm, tanned glow of her skin. It was the London accent that caught Katy's attention; there was an intriguing elegance to it. She made no reply, hoping the woman would think her rude, regret the intrusion and wish her farewell.

"My husband and kids are asleep," Alexina continued, "and it dawned on me that I've never welcomed you to the building. So…"

The neighbour raised her eyebrows and shook the bottle from side to side, an advance Katy felt powerless to stop. She could tell straight away Alexina wasn't the type to accept a negative answer. Almost unconsciously, Katy stood back and opened the door wider, allowing the stranger into her home.

"Is your little one sleeping too?" Alexina asked, as she enthusiastically bounced past Katy into the hallway.

She nodded. "Yes, so let's keep it down. Straight ahead, we can sit in there."

"Don't forget to grab a couple of glasses."

Katy partly closed the living room door, keeping it open just a little in an attempt to guard her son from the unusual noise of conversation. Reluctantly, she accepted the glass of wine and sank back into the sofa while Alexina spoke at an incredibly fast pace.

"I also wanted to say sorry, for the other night. You know… the police and the paramedics. I'm sure they made a racket; no consideration for other people. They just charge in, proverbial guns blazing."

"They came for you?" With two apartments on the floor above, it was interesting to hear a bit of the story. "I guess there was some noise on the stairs, but I didn't see anything."

"No I bet you didn't. You keep yourself very much to yourself, don't you?"

Katy smiled, anxious about the direction the discussion could take. She began to regret letting the woman in. *What if she asks where I'm from, or why I'm a single parent? What if she's here to find information on me and I just let her walk freely into my home?*

"Anyway," Alexina continued. "It was all blown out of proportion. My husband and I had a barney that's all, and the neighbours opposite us called the cops."

"Oh, I see."

"The thing is, my husband works away for weeks at a time, sometimes months. When he comes home our relationship can swing either way. I'm either all over him like a rash until he has to leave again, because well, you know, a woman has needs, or I want to kill him for leaving me alone with a toddler and a daughter who's five going on fifteen."

Katy smiled and buried the paranoia trying to take root in her mind. It was nice to have some real adult company, and she found the woman's easy-going attitude relaxing.

"So, Alexina, where are you from?"

"Ah ha… what, you don't think my complexation matches my South London accent?"

"Sorry. I wasn't being rude… I was just –"

Alexina clapped her hands and laughed. "Lighten up. Well, my mother is from India, moved to London when she was a teenager and met my father who was born and bred in Sutton. They still live there but I got out at sixteen, as I was desperate to travel and see the world. Then I met 'him' upstairs and look at me now, stuck in our own quiet little town. The irony of life, hey."

"It's funny how things work out. I know Sutton, south of the river, but not too far from where I used to live." Katy sipped the wine, immediately regretting how she'd slipped into easy chatter. She hoped Alexina wouldn't catch on to the abrupt halt in her sentence. "I've never really travelled, a couple of low-key holidays, but never too far from home. Where have you been?"

"All over. Nothing better than a long-haul flight to know you're getting away and embarking on a huge adventure. But sadly, I haven't been on a plane since my eldest was born five years ago… Changed my life."

Alexina's eyes fluttered to the floor, a distant expression clouded her face. Katy somehow felt drawn to her, almost as if the woman might somehow understand her pain. But she knew it would be wrong to probe her. Sometimes, people just didn't need to share their sad stories.

"And you've lived here ever since?" Katy asked.

The woman's head sprung up, the jovial character returned. "God no! Like I said, his job moves him around the country and sometimes we have to pack up and move with him."

"That must be hard… So, what does your husband do, I mean, what's his job?"

A high-pitched scream from the next room interrupted the conversation. It was so unlike Frankie to wake during the night, it took Katy a minute to process it was actually her son. She quickly clinked her glass onto the coffee table and ran to him. He was sat up in his bed, rubbing his eyes and whimpering.

"Sweetie, what's wrong?"

"I had a dream, Mummy. There was a stranger here…"

"Shh, shh, shh, darling. It's okay. Mummy's here."

Katy wrapped her arms around Frankie, cradling him gently until he fell back to sleep. She lowered him back onto the pillow and crept away. The living room was empty and the wine bottle had gone. Opening the front door slightly, Katy heard the thud of another one closing upstairs.

CHAPTER SEVEN

As devastated as he was to lose another member of the team, Hamilton could not deny Wedlock's request for compassionate leave. Gathering only Clarke and Fraser together left him feeling uneasy; his team was changing at the rate of knots, and he wasn't enjoying it.

"How's Wedlock's mother, gov?" Clarke asked.

"Not good I'm afraid. He called me when he arrived at the hospital in Cornwall. She'd suffered a major stroke."

"Nasty they are. My grandfather had two of them. She'll need some looking after that's for sure. Wedlock doesn't have any siblings, does he?"

"No. Only child," Hamilton replied. "Fraser, it looks like you'll have to work on this case alone for the time being. Unless you want me to pull a uniform in?"

"It's fine, I can manage, boss. I've secured a list of Paige Everett's friends from her parents, so I'll be busy chasing them down today. Sorry, my full update of the case is on the board."

Hamilton took the sarcastic comment like a punch to the gut, knowing full well he couldn't retaliate against Fraser's snide remark. He wanted to explain why he'd pushed the case away and reassure her it was nothing personal, but there never seemed to be an appropriate moment. It had been a long time since he'd opened up and shared the events of his own heart-break. He wasn't confident the words would flow successfully.

"Good to hear it. Right, Clarke and I –" he was interrupted by the shrill of a phone.

His partner answered the call and Hamilton walked to the alcove in the corner of the office. He cursed when he found there were no teabags or coffee, and nothing but an empty pint of milk sat in the fridge. He reached in and tossed the carton onto the work surface. Feeling Fraser's ever-watchful gaze upon him, he avoided eye contact as he returned to Clarke.

I'm the bloody boss in this office. Maybe I need to remind everyone of that fact.

"Gov, we've got a case. Another mother and son murdered in their beds," Clarke announced after he'd ended the call.

"Got the address?"

"Of course! It's within a five-mile radius of the Mitchell victim's address."

"Grab your coat, I'm driving," Hamilton instructed, and marched through the office.

The short journey to Islington allowed his mind to wonder about the man committing these crimes. The team knew from the preliminary information that their latest victim had been discovered sooner than the first, and Hamilton worried about the repercussions it could spark. Would it anger the killer more if he considered they were ruining his plans? Would it entice the monster to escalate the attacks?

Hamilton was surprised to find himself parking the car outside yet another residential cul-de-sac of apartments. There were just too many people, too many roads and buildings in central London that all looked identical; underground stations surrounded by apartment blocks, offices and shops. He could understand how easy it was to get lost. But, Hamilton was a man of the streets, and he knew these streets well, certainly well enough to decipher how unique they actually were. And so, to be called into a crime scene with a similar MO, victims and home, his intuition screamed at him that these victims had not been chosen by chance.

Entering the ground floor flat, Hamilton was overwhelmed by the life inside; the smell of last night's roast dinner still lingered in the air, damp towels from a late-night bath hung on the corridor radiator and the landing light shone without need. He watched the buzz of activity for a few minutes, the teams of colleagues hurrying from room to room to secure any possible piece of evidence.

Hamilton came together with the same group of people to scrutinise a familiar crime scene – no forced entry, personal possessions left untouched, a half-naked dead woman and a child suffocated in his bed. They were hunting a cold-blooded serial killer, and the world outside fell away. Their dark task of giving the dead a voice fuelled their every action.

On their return to the station, Hamilton requested Clarke update Fraser on their progress with the bedroom killings. It was difficult working two cases with half the people he was used to, and while he expected flexibility from his small team, it was not an issue he was willing to ignore.

Charging into his superior's office, Hamilton stopped at the secretary's desk. "Afternoon, Betty. Any chance I can slip in and talk to DCI Allen briefly?"

"Oh, I'm not sure, Denis. He's only just returned to the office," the attractive, mature woman informed him, but made no attempt to get up and physically stop him.

"Cheers," he replied with a wink.

He pounded on the office door and entered when the DCI barked something inaudible. Hamilton was taken aback to find his superior in sweaty gym clothes. Never before had he seen DCI Allen out of his pristine uniform.

"Ah, Denis! Take a seat. You've caught me on a late lunch-break," Allen said, gesturing with his hands over his attire. "What can I do for you?"

"We've just attended a second crime scene of a mother and son murdered in their homes, sir."

"Yes, I was going to give you a call about that. Give me a brief update." The large man wiped his face with a towel and sat in the chair opposite Hamilton.

"Well, sir, unlike the first victims, Emma Jones and her son, Kyle, were found just days after they were attacked. Miss Bairden, who was an old friend of the victim, was visiting and found their bodies. We've scheduled an interview with her tomorrow."

"What about the first victims?"

"Quite the opposite, sir." Hamilton blew a puff of air. "We're having trouble finding any family. There's no information on Miss Mitchell's next of kin at the moment."

"Any link between the victims?"

Hamilton had expected these questions, but he just wished the chief would back off for a minute and let him explain why he had rushed in to see him.

"Not at the moment, sir. I've just returned from the scene and my team are working with fewer numbers. However, the two women were similar in looks and age, lived within a mile of each other, both single parents with young sons –"

"Right! Those families need to be informed, and we need to release a press statement, Denis. For now, I'll do my best to ensure the press team are instructed to keep the victims' names away from the headlines."

Allen rose from his seat and crossed the office in three large strides. Before he was dismissed, Hamilton quickly interjected.

"Sir, there was something else."

"Yes, Denis?"

"You realise I'm two members short on my team, don't you, sir?"

"I'm working on it. There's been a delay with Dixon's transfer, the sergeant replacing Morris."

"I understand these things happen, sir." Hamilton clenched his jaw for a moment, keeping his frustration at bay. "But you must also understand that we're working on two major investigations here. I will need to use Fraser's computer skills if I'm to uncover a connection with these two women, but she's stuck working on the… teenager's death."

Allen dropped his fingers from the door handle. "I thought DI Daly had been assigned that case?"

"You informed me he had been called to another crime scene that same evening, sir, and requested I attend in his place."

The man cleared his throat. "Denis, my apologies…"

Hamilton shook his head. "No need, sir, we're all professionals. I'm just asking for some help for my team until the new guy arrives. I'm not sure when Wedlock will return from his compassionate leave."

He walked to the door, side-stepping Allen, and pulled at the collar of his shirt. It wasn't a small office, but it was suddenly consumed with thick, hot air.

"Say no more, Denis. I'll have someone transferred to your team as soon as possible."

Hamilton bowed his head in thanks and dashed from the office, through the corridors and out into the car park before anyone had a chance to engage him in a conversation he still wasn't prepared to have.

CHAPTER EIGHT

Fraser drove along Kilburn High Road, replaying in her mind the earlier interaction with her boss. Hamilton had seemed distracted over the past fortnight. Granted she hadn't worked with him for as long as Clarke, and he appeared to be carrying on as normal, but something niggled at the back of her mind. It was something to do with the case she was working on, of that she was certain. What she couldn't decide was whether or not to question him about it. The relaxed office environment had disappeared, the team spirit had lost its heart and she wanted to alter things. What she didn't want to do was make enemies in the first six months. She cranked up the radio, hoping Kisstory's tunes would drown out her thoughts.

This is definitely a perk of working alone; no one to dictate the music choices.

As Fraser approached Cricklewood Lane, she indicated right and parked on Elm Grove. From home to home, this was the closest in distance to one of Paige Everett's friends. Despite the circumstances, Fraser couldn't help but smile when Mrs Everett had described the girl as her daughter's best friend. She hoped the special title was worthy of this girl and she'd turn out to be an asset to the investigation.

Fraser knocked on the door and waited with her ID badge in hand. Bellowing words and footsteps came from behind the panelled glass doorway until a shadowy figure drew near. A short, slim woman, wearing a Breton stripe top and jeans, answered the door; pale but naturally pretty, with close-cropped hair that Fraser thought added to the woman's elegant style.

"Yes?"

"Mrs Sarah Steer?"

"Who's asking?"

"Detective Sergeant Kerry Fraser from the Metropolitan Police. Is Caitlynn Steer your daughter?"

"Yes. Is this about Paige?"

Fraser nodded. "Could I speak to Caitlynn, ma'am?"

"Of course, I'm sorry. Come on in. Can I get you a drink?"

"No thank you, I –"

"Caitlynn! Caitlynn, love, get downstairs right this instant," Mrs Steer called from the hallway. "Follow me into the kitchen, Detective. I'll put the kettle on."

Fraser walked behind the woman, glancing at the walls adorned with photographs of family and friends. She entered the large kitchen. The patio doors opened onto a well-kept garden.

"Large family?" she said, thumbing back towards the photos in the hallway.

"Isn't everyone's?"

Mrs Steer smiled, and busied herself collecting the mugs and spoons and boiled the kettle. Fraser didn't want to sound rude by turning down her hospitality again, so allowed the woman to continue.

"How has Caitlynn been since Paige's death?"

"How do you think, Detective? They were the very best of friends, you know." Fraser nodded, but sensed the woman hadn't finished. "She's been in an awful state, barely said a word and hasn't eaten a morsel, I'm telling you. I just don't know what to do… how can I help her? The poor Everett family, they're lovely people… and I haven't had the heart to pay them a visit. That's disgusting behaviour, isn't it? Oh, Caitlynn, darling. Here she is, Detective."

Fraser turned to find a young girl hunched over and looking aimlessly around the room. From her notes, she knew Caitlynn had turned sixteen already but the girl's elfin physique coupled with a swollen, tear-stained face made her look more thirteen, if that.

"Hello, Caitlynn. My name is Kerry, I work for the Police. Could I have a chat with you about Paige?"

"You've... you've seen it... haven't you?" the girl whispered.

Fraser crouched down low to the floor and gazed up to Caitlynn. "Seen what?"

"I didn't think she'd really go through with it. Honestly, I didn't! If I had known... I would have..." A stream of tears erupted from Caitlynn's eyes.

"What are you talking about, darling?" Mrs Steer uttered.

"Caitlynn, come and take a seat for me," Fraser instructed, and led the girl to the table. "Now, can you explain what it is you're talking about?"

"I can't... I'll get in trouble."

"Caitlynn Steer, you tell the detective this minute what's going on."

"Please, Mrs Steer your tone of voice isn't helping. I don't want Caitlynn to feel like she's in trouble and... actually, I'd really love that cup of tea now."

The woman pinched her lips together, but said no more. Making more noise than necessary, it was obvious to Fraser that Mrs Steer was still listening to their conversation.

"Now, Caitlynn, I want you to know I'm here to help you. And I'm here for Paige too. It's important you tell me what you know."

"He dared her." The girl hesitated for a few moments. "He said if she took the drugs he'd go on a date with her. He was lying, of course he was, just leading her on so him and his friends had another excuse to take the piss out of us," Caitlynn blurted.

Fraser took a deep breath and thought back to the crime scene; Mr and Mrs Everett were right to proclaim Paige's death was not a suicide.

"Can you tell me who *he* is? We'll protect you, and you will not get into trouble, Caitlynn. But we need to know who was involved, for your best friend's sake."

The girl lifted her head and looked Fraser in the eye for the first time. She wondered if it had been a low blow, if the young girl actually had some fire inside and would tell Fraser where she could stick her protection.

"Billy. Billy Roscoe. He's a few years older than us, in the sixth form college attached to our school. We thought we'd get a break from them all during the holidays, but they followed us. When we were shopping at Brent Cross, they'd be there. Or if we went to the cinema at the outlet, they'd be there too. They always knew where we were."

Caitlynn cupped her hands over her face, her shoulders shaking with silent tears. Fraser felt the pain of losing a friend to drugs; the only difference was this had been a tragic accident.

"You thought I had seen something, Caitlynn. What were you referring to?"

The girl used the sleeve of her jumper to wipe the mingled tears and snot away. "The video… on Facebook. Billy's one condition to taking Paige out was that she had to take the drugs live. He said he wanted to watch her."

"Did Billy give Paige the drugs?"

Caitlynn nodded. "She called me earlier that day saying he had been round her house and gave her a bag of some white powder. He said all she had to do was sniff it live on Facebook and he'd take her to the cinema the next night. Paige is… was… my best friend. She just wanted to have her first date… she just wanted Billy to like her."

The girl lowered her head to the table and wailed. Mrs Steer dashed to her daughter's side, bundling her in her arms and cried with her.

"Caitlynn, had Paige ever taken drugs before?" The girl shook her head and continued to sob. "Thank you for speaking with me. You've really helped Paige's case. Mrs Steer, we will need Caitlynn to make an official statement. But, for now, thank you, I'll see myself out."

Fraser left the house and sat quietly in the car for a few moments, suppressing the overwhelming sadness inside.

Before returning to the station, she made a detour to the mortuary. Since joining the team, there'd been no need for her to visit the pathologist in charge of the investigations. That was something Hamilton always dealt with, sometimes sending Morris and Wedlock, which she was thankful for – unsure if she had the stomach for that element of the job yet. Hoping to pick up the results from Audrey Gibson, and not to witness the live examination of a young corpse, it was clear whatever the outcome she was on her own with this case. She took a deep breath and headed off in search of the woman's office.

"Hello, Miss Gibson? I'm DS Fraser."

"Please, call me Audrey, and don't stand on ceremony in the doorway. Come in and have a seat. Do you have a first name, or is it politically correct to call everyone by their surname?"

"It's common practice I suppose, surname or nickname," Fraser explained. "But, it's Kerry."

"I'm new to this team… is it easy to tell?" The woman smiled.

"Well, that makes two of us. Although I won't be for much longer…" Fraser stopped, preventing herself from rambling any further. "I was hoping to get some information on an investigation I'm leading. I'm sorry to come unannounced. Should I have called first?"

"Yes, I think it's quite formal here. But I prefer to work in a relaxed atmosphere, so feel free to call or pop in whenever you like. Which case are you referring to?"

"Paige Everett, the young teenager. Suspected overdose."

Audrey rifled through a stack of different coloured folders on her desk, swaying to a tune she hummed aloud, her scarlet hair swishing around her shoulders as she moved.

"Ah ha, here it is! Paige Everett, sudden cardiac death," Audrey announced. "The toxicology report showed presence of cocaine in the victim's system."

"Her friend said it was the first time Paige had taken drugs."

"Sadly, that doesn't always matter, Kerry. There's no way of knowing the purity of cocaine because it's commonly mixed with other compounds, such as aspirin and other over-the-counter medications. Plus, your victim suffered from asthma."

Fraser frowned. "What influence would that have had?"

"Cocaine reduces the flow of oxygen to the heart, forcing the muscle to work harder and causing the user's breathing to weaken. This would have put immense pressure on the long-term condition already affecting Paige's airways. Some asthma sufferers have a sensitivity to anti-inflammatory drugs, such as aspirin –"

"Which could have been mixed with the cocaine," Fraser finished the sentence.

"Exactly."

"And that escalated to a sudden cardiac? Sorry, I feel quite ignorant asking that. I guess I've just always assumed it was more of an addiction thing and it's the regular use of these drugs that would have caused a fatal overdose."

"In most cases that would be true, but Paige Everett was very unlucky. A sudden cardiac death is caused by abnormal heart rhythms called arrhythmias. It may be more detail than you need, but it basically means it's when a person's normal rhythm becomes irregular. Paige's heart rate became so slow it didn't pump enough blood to meet her body's needs. Again, certain anti-inflammatory drugs can trigger this."

"Would Paige have known she had a sensitivity to aspirin?"

"Yes, I would have imagined so. What she probably wouldn't have known was if the cocaine contained it. But, Kerry, you have to understand all of this is indeterminate and the victim's samples have been sent for more sophisticated tests."

Fraser sighed heavily, once again controlling the melancholy she felt for the young girl. "How wretched."

"I'll admit, I'm usually a guarded person when it comes to death, it's the nature of my job, but this has troubled me. It's the awful irony of it all. Some people will abuse drugs for years and this inexperienced teenager died after her first time. I hope you catch the scum who sold it to her."

"Yes… I will, Audrey. Thanks for helping me understand the science of it."

The woman smiled. "That's my job. Maybe you'd like to attend a live post-mortem one day? You'll get a feel for how the procedure and process works, and understand why it can take so long for us to get back to you. It's really not because we're holding out on the info."

Fraser froze, glaring at Audrey. She wanted to explain it wasn't part of the job she was ready to undertake, that it was one thing to see a dead body at a crime scene for a short period of time, but she'd heard some post-mortems could take hours. Just the thought of what the room might smell like, and hands rummaging around to extract internal organs, already made her shudder.

Audrey chuckled. "Okay, Kerry I won't push you. But if you're ever ready, the offer is there. Perhaps we could go for a drink some time though? A few of the friendships are quite tight around here, and I haven't found a place I can slot into yet."

"Yeah, I'd love that," she replied; a drink was something Fraser could handle.

CHAPTER NINE

Katy and Frankie returned home from another afternoon in the park, and Katy was looking forward to chilling out for a few hours before her night shift at the pub. As the key slipped in the front door, she heard Alexina's voice call down to her. There wasn't enough time to race inside and lock the door; she could hear the woman's footsteps descending the stairs.

"Hey, neighbour! Why didn't you answer me earlier?"

She turned to face her without removing the key from the top lock. "When?"

"I knocked a few hours ago."

"We've been out since lunchtime."

Alexina turned her attention to Frankie. "Hello, cutie. Aren't you just adorable! Anyway, it was about two o'clock, and I'd come down to tell you the husband has left on his travels again. Could be gone at least a month this time. Your flat was quiet, but I could have sworn I heard you walking about."

"No, we were definitely in the park all afternoon."

"My imagination's playing tricks on me again, I suppose." Alexina laughed, and peered back up the stairs. "Look, why don't you come up to mine for dinner and a sleepover tonight?"

"I'm working tonight, but thank you."

"Ah, well come up for your dinner anyway before you go then. I make a mean spaghetti bolognaise. Frankie can meet the girls too… wouldn't he love some playmates?"

Katy gripped the key tighter in her hand, a voice inside telling her to thank the woman, decline and return to the safety of their home. Chatting on the stairwell was not a highly-ranked pastime in her book. She looked down at her son, who didn't beg, or throw a tantrum to get what he wanted, but his blue eyes widened with excitement. He silently pleaded, and her heart melted.

"It's a really kind offer, Alexina. We'd love to."

"Awesome, come on up," the women said, bouncing back up the stairs two at a time. "The girls are playing in their room, Frankie."

"Oh my gosh! Thank you, Mum. I'm so excited," he yelled, and followed Alexina.

Katy retrieved her keys and slipped them back into the pocket of her jeans, resigned to the fact her son's need for friends exceeded her own desire to be alone.

"You scarpered off pretty fast the other night." Katy joined Alexina in the kitchen, once she'd seen Frankie settled with Lily and Nancy in their princess-pink bedroom.

"Well, you know how it is… when one of my girls wakes in the night, I could be in with them for hours singing lullabies and hugging them back to sleep. Thought I'd duck out and leave you to it. Hmm… try this."

Alexina lifted a spoon filled with bolognaise to Katy's lips. Not one to don an apron, she'd forgotten how comforting a tasty dish could be, and decided she and Frankie deserved to have a nice meal and some company for a change. It couldn't do any harm.

The hours passed, and Katy found herself disappointed with work looming on the horizon. She had enjoyed herself more than expected; Alexina loved to share her adventure stories and Katy enjoyed hearing them. Frankie had hardly made an appearance; the new trio of friends remained busy with their imaginative games of teachers and doctors and patients.

"Feel free to pop up whenever you like, Katy. I'm pretty much always at home." Alexina laughed.

"Please can I sleepover, Mum?" Frankie peeked from around the bedroom door. "We're not finished with our game."

"But Samantha will be over soon to babysit."

"Mum, please? Please! P-p-p-lease?"

Lily and Nancy's heads appeared under his at the door and she couldn't help but laugh at the bobbing children, all smiling eagerly. Katy had taken her son away from so much since moving from London, and his lack of friendships was through no fault of his own. Katy sighed with guilt. Shrugging, she looked at Alexina to help make the decision.

"Hey, it's fine with me. He's a good boy, I know he won't be any trouble."

Once again that evening, Katy broke. "Okay you can stay. I'll pop downstairs, call the babysitter and grab Frankie's pyjamas before I head to work."

The cheers of jubilation echoed even after Alexina had closed the door behind her. Though the nerves bubbled in her stomach like an erupting volcano, she knew that if they were truly going to make a new life for themselves here, then she had to relax and allow Frankie these opportunities.

After calling Samantha to offer the babysitter her fee, which the young girl graciously refused, Katy became frustrated at having misplaced her favourite lip gloss. Not wanting to be late, she gave up the search and nipped back upstairs. Mobile numbers were swapped between the two women and Frankie was caught in a suffocating hug. Only then was Katy finally ready to walk to work.

"Penny for them... you look preoccupied," John said from the other side of the bar.

Katy was momentarily caught off-guard by his uncharacteristic attention and continued to pull the pint of bitter. She almost admitted how uneasy she'd felt about Frankie staying with a stranger, and how the only thing keeping her from falling apart was knowing he was not far from her, but she needed to restrain herself; this was work, not a counselling session.

"Aren't we all, John?" she replied, and laughed.

"Aye, you're not wrong there, lass." He paid for his pint and returned to his newspaper.

Four patrons filled the entire bar, and Katy's comfortable status quo returned. Content that everyone's glasses were filled, the tables were cleaned and the outside ashtrays emptied, she perched herself at the end of the bar with her Kindle. Having endured enough loss and fear, she avoided all types of crime thrillers and clicked the button to her favourite Marissa Farrar book, losing herself in a world of spirit shifters.

"Hey, Katy!" her boss called out, as he entered the bar from his office. "I've just ordered your taxi but Pete wasn't on shift. They said they'll try and get you a female driver instead."

"Thanks, Craig."

"Go on, you head off and wait outside. I'll clear this lot up."

Katy bid her boss farewell and went out the back to collect her jacket and bag from the stockroom. She was delighted to read a text from Alexina, discovering Frankie and the girls had worn themselves out and were in bed by ten p.m. She fired off a thank-you reply text, promising to see them all for breakfast. It was a later time than she usually let her son stay awake, but for the first time in a long time, happiness triumphed over anxiety.

She stood at the side staff entrance and waited for the taxi. Nothing came. Katy knew better than to call for a progress report on the driver's journey; growing up in London taught her that the taxi controller's answer would always be 'just five more minutes,' regardless of where the car actually was. It was now half-past midnight, and she took comfort in the fact Samantha wasn't at her house waiting to leave. Swinging her bag over her shoulder, Katy marched off in the direction of home. *Everything happens for a reason.*

In what now felt like a former life, top hair stylist Katy loved the craziness of London. You couldn't walk two minutes without seeing another face; they could be any race or religion, dressed in a formal suit or making a statement with colourful fashion. You never knew what you'd find in the city and you were never alone. It was something Katy had loved about London, and the hair salon offered more gossip and laughs than a soap opera ever could have. But, when she became the brunt of the rumours and jokes, she had to escape; she couldn't face those strangers any more.

Living in Hertfordshire was like a holiday for her; it was quiet and unassuming, unquestioningly peaceful. Walking alone, she passed dark houses where families slept peacefully in their beds. The lamp posts lit her way along the well-groomed hedges and blossoming flowers. To start her life afresh, she'd only travelled twenty-five miles, but it felt like a different country. Katy walked onto her road, where her apartment block was just about visible at the end of the street, and smiled to herself, contentment radiating over her.

The slow drag of footsteps from behind Katy forced her to spin around. Despite the black sky, she knew who stood in front of her. It was a heavy build she knew too well. He raised his hands and closed the gap between them. Bile rose in her throat as a single tear tumbled down her face.

"Look, love, I just want to talk to you. Please don't be afraid," Brad said.

He walked further towards her, out of the shadows. She was unable to ignore the scar trailing from the end of his eyebrow to the tip of his ear. The mental command to formulate any words ignored, Katy could only respond by shaking her head.

"Please, listen," he whined. "I've sorted myself out. You can come home, I need you and Frankie in my life."

Katy's noiseless tears rolled freely. "How...how did you –"

"How did I find you? Sweetheart, I've always known where you were." They stood face to face, so close their breath mingled in the air. "Do you really think I'd ever let you leave me?"

"But... it's been... I left... How?" Katy stumbled back onto the waist-high wall of the house behind her. Her eyes urgently roamed the sleepy street.

Brad took another step forward, his legs slipped in-between hers, and he stroked her face. "I put a tracking device on your mobile phone last year. When you turned it on I came straight here, but I could see you were still upset for doing this to me." He pointed to the mutilation on his face, and smiled. "I thought I'd let you have this little holiday with Frankie, take some time to forgive yourself."

The wet stream of tears scorched her cheeks, and Katy's fear turned to fury. She stood up straight, forcing her husband away from her.

"I was protecting my son! I will never, ever regret what I did to you."

Brad gave a low whistle and nodded his head. "I see the feisty side of my wife is in control of that mouthpiece tonight. Turns me on when you get all gutsy."

"You animal, get lost! We stayed away from you because you're a monster... a bully. I don't deserve to be treated that way, to be scared in my own home, by my own husband."

"Oh please, woman," he snapped. "You'd be nothing without me. I gave you a home, a job, a son, a reason to exist. If it weren't for me, you'd still be snivelling your sorrows about your dead parents, sticking your nose in that white stuff."

Katy's eyes widened. "How dare you? That happened once. Five bloody years ago," she yelled, enraged more at herself for failing to find a safe haven for Frankie.

From nowhere, another man stood by Brad. There was something oddly familiar about the stranger's dark eyes.

"Is everything okay here?" he asked, in a soft tone.

Brad turned away from Katy and glared at the man. "Fuck off, mate. This doesn't concern you."

Her husband drew back his shoulders and Katy, now confident they weren't friends, caught the man's gaze and silently pleaded for his help.

Brad shoved the man's chest. "You deaf or what? Keep moving."

Within seconds the two men were shouting obscenities and scuffling with each other. Katy didn't wait to discover who had the upper hand, but instead sprinted off towards her home.

CHAPTER TEN

Hamilton placed a white, polystyrene cup into the woman's shaky hands. Her chestnut curls fell unbrushed around a face drained of colour, the only exception was the redness in her eyes. He overlooked the grief, the need to launch forward with the investigation compelling him.

"Miss Bairden, I understand you're probably very tired and want to get home, so we'll do this as quickly as we can."

"It's fine, I want to help. And you can call me Lynn."

"How did you know the victims, Emma Jones and her son, Kyle?"

She sniffed, roughly wiping her nose with a well-used tissue and took a deep breath. "When I was a teenager I moved from Scotland to study at King's College London University. Emma was so confident and vibrant, and I just felt like a country bumpkin. Being local, she gave me a tour of the city, and showed me all the good clubs and where to shop, and we've been friends ever since... Sixteen years..."

The woman's eyes glazed over, staring into Hamilton's chest as though she was looking right through him and into the past. He noted the lack of control Lynn held over her own emotions but, tearful as she was, she continued her story.

"I hadn't seen Emma for just over four years. I never met Kyle. She sent me photos of him growing up and we spoke on the phone, but, well, I didn't like her husband, Tony. They'd married just a few months after meeting each other and Emma changed. She was no longer the bright woman I'd met all those years before. Anyway, there was no love lost between Tony and I, and he apparently thought I encouraged too much socialising and partying. Soon enough, Emma was pregnant and she said we couldn't see each other anymore."

"So, what prompted this visit, Lynn?" Hamilton asked.

"We kept in touch, via email and text. I assumed she'd done it in secret and I never asked... I didn't want the messages to stop again. Then, one day she called and told me she had finally left Tony. I could hear the happiness in her voice. There was a restraining order against him, Emma had a new apartment and Kyle was in nursery." Lynn widened her eyes and gasped. "Oh, my God, it was him. That bastard killed them."

"Let's just calm down for a minute," Hamilton said. "This is the first we've heard of Miss Jones's husband. Tell us everything you know about him, and Emma's other relatives. I promise you we'll investigate every angle of this case."

Hamilton and Clarke spent the next thirty minutes with Lynn, delving into everything she knew about Tony Jones. It was more progress than they had made with Scarlett Mitchell and her son, Noah; their stench of death still lingered in his nostrils, and was a stark reminder of his failure. Knowing the forensic results could take some time with those first victims, he was desperate to obtain as much information as possible; confident if he found a link between the two women it would be the key to unmasking their killer.

"You're deep in thought, gov," Clarke said as the pair watched Lynn leave the station.

He mumbled a reply, made his way through reception and took the stairs up to the incident room.

"Look, gov, we could really do with Fraser on this case. Her keyboard wizardry is second to none, and it would free me up a bit to dig into the family, get out and interview... Gov, are you listening?"

"Yeah." He turned in the stairwell and looked at his partner. "I'll see how Fraser's doing, but I've already spoken to the chief about the situation."

"About the other case –"

"Leave it, Clarke."

Hamilton continued to climb the stairs, frustrated his concentration was being pulled elsewhere. He appreciated certain matters needed to be confronted, especially the clash with Fraser; they had to move on from this and work the case. A storm brewed inside his mind, the dull pain ran from his temples and down his neck – mainly when he thought about his personal life clashing with the professional.

In the incident room, Hamilton cursed himself for not stopping at the canteen and made a mental note to replenish the refreshments in the office kitchen. Fraser continued to tap away at her keyboard, never making eye contact with her colleagues. He asked her to join them at the evidence boards where Clarke was busy updating the information.

"Right, we need you on this case with us," Hamilton said. "I'm going to have another word with DCI –"

"No need to do that, boss," Fraser interrupted.

He frowned, waiting for her to continue. Apparently, she didn't intend on divulging any further information voluntarily and so, unimpressed with the volatile course their relationship had taken, Hamilton probed further.

"And why is that, Fraser? How did your interviews go yesterday?"

"They went very well, boss. Paige Everett did not commit suicide, but was goaded into snorting cocaine live on Facebook. I've just requested that the video be removed from the social media site."

"It was still on there? Did you watch it?" Hamilton clenched his fists.

"Yes, as were all the comments from those who watched it. I did watch it, boss. It was sickening…" Fraser closed her eyes briefly, before pulling herself a little straighter. "Anyway, the outcome is that uniform accompanied me this morning to arrest the dealer, Billy Roscoe. He's in custody now and the case has been passed over to CID."

"Good work. Has this all been cleared with the chief?"

"No, it hasn't… I thought it best to inform you first."

"I'll update him. You should be proud of yourself."

"Actually, boss, would you mind if I saw DCI Allen? I'd like to wrap up this case myself."

It wasn't usual procedure to allow a detective sergeant to report to the chief, but Hamilton recognised there was a possibility he had failed Fraser when he'd jumped ship on the investigation. He wanted to rebuild the close working relationship they'd had previously and granted her request.

An agonising fervour gripped him, and the urge to advance with the bedroom murders felt crucial. Hamilton asked his partner to bring Fraser up to speed and, always happy to take the floor, Clarke sprang into action.

"Here's what we've got: The two crime scenes are within a five-mile radius of each other, Pimlico and Islington. The females were both in their early thirties, their sons aged four and five, and all four were murdered in their homes. In their beds. At the moment, we can only guesstimate, but it looks likely that the two families were killed at least two months apart. We're waiting for confirmation on cause of death but, with Scarlett Mitchell, that could take some time considering how advanced her body had decomposed. We're probably looking at a sexual crime given the position of the bodies, and they were both naked from the waist down."

"There isn't much information about the first victim, Miss Mitchell," Fraser said pointing at the evidence board.

"That's because we don't know much about her yet."

Hamilton stood up and crossed his arms. "And there's where I want your attention, Fraser. Get me everything you can on this woman and her son. Clarke, you do the same with the Jones family so we can determine how these women link up."

"If they do at all, gov," Clarke replied. "Sometimes people are just in the wrong place at the wrong time."

"Hmm, I don't know. They just seem too similar for there not to be a connection."

"How did the perpetrator get into the homes, boss?" Fraser asked.

"From what the forensics team gathered at the crime scenes, there was no forced entry or opened windows at either of the houses."

"Well, in that case, I don't think it was sheer bad luck, Clarke. The women might have invited the attacker into their homes, or he was skilled enough to get in and out undetected."

Hamilton slowly slid his index finger back and forth over his closed lips, contemplating what Fraser had just said. His eyes scanned over the evidence boards, the crime scene photographs and every minute detail before him.

"Both these women were lonely. Scarlett was left undiscovered for weeks, and I'd say Emma was headed for the same fate if it wasn't for an irregular visit from an old friend… Right, change of plan! Fraser, I want you to delve into both women's lives and cross-reference for similar support groups, be that divorced or single mothers, and any comparable online activity. Clarke, there's CCTV everywhere in London, I want you to find out if there's any cameras in or around the buildings the victims lived in. I'll hunt down this Tony Jones. Let's find out why his wife had a restraining order against him."

Fraser and Clarke shared an inaudible joke as they returned to their desks. The tension had broken for now, and Hamilton felt as though he had regained some form of control. He wasn't prepared to let his collapsed resolve hinder his role and endanger another family in their homes.

CHAPTER ELEVEN

The following morning, Katy sat at the small kitchen table in Alexina's flat, nursing her fourth cup of coffee. She had never seen her son so happy and couldn't believe he still wanted to spend time with his two new friends. While the children were busy watching a film, Katy confided in her new, friendly neighbour about the previous night's event.

"That must have been terrifying! Are you hurt? You should have come straight up here; did you get any sleep last night?" Alexina questioned.

"No. I sat in the hallway with a baseball bat in one hand and a kitchen knife in the other. I really thought he would have come to the house."

"Bloody hell, Katy! Why didn't you call the police if you were that scared?"

"I can't. They'll take Frankie away from me."

Alexina reached her hand across the table and took Katy's. "Why? What happened, love?"

She glanced over her shoulder. The children were laughing hysterically at a scene from Toy Story, oblivious to their mother's conversation. Katy bowed her head, knowing this was the only chance she might have to trust someone, but unsure whether or not to take the risk. Alexina withdrew her hand and waited silently. She finally looked up and met her friend's gaze.

"Brad is a violent man... we married too soon. I never really knew who he was, but I was in such a dark place after my parents died, I thought he had rescued me from all of that. It was little things at first, he'd accuse me of flirting and call me names, and then he started controlling the money and who I spent time with.

It got worse after Frankie's first birthday. He watched every little thing I did. I started getting a taxi home from work every day because I was petrified of what would happen if I was late, and his dinner wasn't ready for him. You know, most of the time he didn't hit me at all, he just had to look at me… his eyes… deep pools of darkness. He was aggressive and rough in the bedroom, frightening even, and I had no one else to turn to. The night we ran away… he had hit Frankie. Brad's huge hand whacked around my little boy's head so hard, his body was tossed to the floor. I didn't think he was going to stop, so I went for him. I kicked and punched and grabbed whatever I could. Until finally, I swung a glass vase and smashed it into his face. There was blood everywhere. He was furious, thumped me so hard in the stomach I could hardly breathe. He said Social Services would take Frankie away from me for what I'd done to him. The next time he left the house, I grabbed my son and we ran."

Katy fumbled with a stray piece of wool on the cuff of her jumper and exhaled slowly; her honesty exhausting.

"Sweetie, you have to go to the police –"

"No! I have no proof, Alexina. He's the one with a huge scar on his face. I'll get arrested and then…"

"It was self-defence. And with him following you here, tracking you with that app, and attacking you in the street, they'll have to believe you."

Katy sighed. "I don't know… I feel so drained. I thought I had taken Frankie away from him. I thought we were safe here. I can't…"

"So, what now? You're just going to give up? Let him come and take you back to that life, or just sit here in fear waiting for another attack?"

"We'll move. I've destroyed the phone last night, he won't be able to find us again."

"Can you guarantee that he won't? And do you really want to spend your life running? Do you really want that to be Frankie's life? You'll be forever looking over your shoulder. Katy, you've already proved you're a fighter. You are strong enough to take your life back. Do it again, but do it properly this time. Stop alienating yourself, you're not on your own any more. I'll come with you to the police station if you want."

Katy smiled, she couldn't remember the last time someone had encouraged her to speak out and be heard. The past few years of her life had been consumed with hiding from the truth, putting on a show for her colleagues and Brad's friends and family; no one had cared about her. She looked across at Alexina and wondered if this stranger could really help her rebuild her life. Could she honestly trust someone again after what she'd been through? She stood up from the table and crossed the hallway to the living room. Standing in the doorway, she watched Frankie. He looked relaxed and carefree, and she knew she would do anything to let him keep this life. Alexina approached from behind.

"You're right," Katy said, and faced her friend. "I can't keep running. It's not much, but I've made a home for us here and only I can keep it safe. I now know Brad has always been aware of where we were… I can't live in fear every day any more."

"That's the spirit," Alexina said.

"Before my shift at The Tavern tonight, I'm going to the police station and telling them everything about Brad. This is my life and I'm taking it back."

"There's one thing you need to do first."

Katy frowned. "What?"

"Go and get some bloody sleep, you look awful!" Alexina laughed. "There's no connection between you and me, so you're both safe here. Have a lie down on my bed, and a shower when you wake up, you'll feel more comfortable."

Without thinking, Katy threw her arms around Alexina and thanked the woman for her kindness. She didn't know if it was the fatigue or the unexpected compassion, but a dizziness soon took hold of her and she welcomed sleep like an old friend.

The police station was only a twenty-minute walk from The Tavern and, with the evening sun still shining, Katy decided to walk to work. Frankie was already asleep by the time she called Alexina to update her on PC Lakhani and the statement she'd given him.

She thought him cute, younger than her with boyish good looks, and yet extremely professional. Katy made her complaint against Brad, and insisted he was a danger to her and her son. Alexina had suggested she omit the glass vase incident for now and concentrate on the fact he was stalking her. PC Lakhani assured Katy someone would look into her case and be in touch with her, but in the meantime, he handed her an abundance of support group leaflets and helpline information.

Satisfied with the decision she'd made, and knowing the police would now help her, enticed a feeling of freedom Katy wasn't expecting. She bounced through the back door of the pub, hung her handbag in its usual place and made her way through to the bar. Craig was by her side instantly, but not before she glimpsed a familiar face on the other side of the bar.

"Hi, Katy, love. I can't stay and chat as I've got a meeting in town. If I don't leave now I'll be late. I'll be back before midnight, don't worry," he said, and he marched through the pub.

The football match played on the lone TV in the corner and had the attention of the only other two patrons. She gazed at them momentarily; they held no interest in the stranger approaching the bar.

"So, it's Katy. I'm Matthew Webb," he said, and outstretched his hand.

She accepted, and briefly shook it, but all the while a voice screamed inside her head. Her heart raced and she could feel beads of sweat escaping the pores of her scalp.

"Listen, about last night –"

"What are you doing here?" Katy interrupted.

"I wanted to see if you were okay?"

"How do you know where I work?" Heat rose from her chest, over her neck and settled on her cheeks like a blazing fire.

"Sorry, I should explain myself."

Matthew sat down on a stool at the bar, making them level and forcing Katy to stare into those brown eyes again. A tug of war struggled in her mind – one side telling her to panic and grab the attention of the regulars, and the other side intrigued by the man who had saved her.

"I'm new to the area and live just around the corner," Matthew continued. "I was here once before, there was a wake. I wasn't part of it, that was simply a coincidence, but it was much busier than tonight... so, you probably didn't notice me. Then, when I saw that man harassing you in the street last night, and I recognised your face from here, I couldn't just walk by without stepping in. I'm sorry if I got involved in a domestic, but I just wanted to make sure you were okay."

Katy's face continued to burn and her stomach clenched. Although the man was tall and muscular, there was something soft about his handsome face, and she couldn't help but smile.

"Don't be sorry, it was definitely a case of right place, right time. Thank you for stepping in. What can I get you? It's on me."

"Cheers, I'll have a pint of Fosters please. So, that jackass was a complete stranger trying his luck?"

She groaned. "No… My ex."

"Ah, tough break-up?"

Katy nodded and placed his pint of beer on the bar. "Did you manage to see where he went after I left?"

"He scrambled about on the floor for a while, obviously pretty drunk. Once I saw you'd made it away, I left him to it and walked home myself."

"Well, thank you again anyway," she said.

Katy emptied the dishwasher of glasses. A nervousness trembled through her body, driving the need to keep herself moving. She could feel Matthew's eyes watching her as she busied herself around the bar. John silently motioned for another drink before turning back to the TV, and she was grateful for his timing.

"Have you worked here long?" Matthew asked.

"Not really, a few weeks."

"You look like a natural behind there."

"So, what brings you to Hertfordshire?" she asked, eager to turn the attention away from herself.

"Oh, you know the usual, work."

Her shift slipped away while Matthew sat in the same spot enjoying two pints, but declining a third. While it was part of the job to chat with the patrons, talking all night was uncommon for Katy, and yet speaking to Matthew felt so easy. When Craig returned at eleven thirty to help prepare for lock up, Matthew offered to wait and walk her home.

"That's sweet of you, thanks, but I'll call a taxi."

"You didn't last night," he said tilting his head to one side, a mischievous expression on his face. "Let me walk you home, it's no trouble."

"Honestly, there's no need. Thank you."

He held his hands up. "Okay, okay. I'm not one to push, just promise me no more walking home alone in the dark."

"Trust me, I won't be doing that again."

Matthew slid a business card onto the bar and smiled with a shrug. "In case you want to meet up for dinner, or lunch, or coffee. You know, whatever suits you. My mobile number is on there."

The invitation fell from his mouth and he couldn't make eye contact with her. Katy nibbled her bottom lip, watching him leave, and supressed a giggle as she tucked the card into her back pocket.

CHAPTER TWELVE

Five years ago

Denis Hamilton parked his car in the driveway and turned the ignition off. He sat in the darkness and soaked up the silence; there was no rush to get inside. The house brought so much uncertainty with it, and he never knew if he'd be greeted with a suffocating quietness or a barrage of aggressive insults. A few extra moments in the car were calming and free. The net curtain in the living room twitched, and he knew he'd been busted. Groaning, Hamilton hauled himself from the vehicle and opened the front door to his home.

No delicious smell of food cooking welcomed him, mainly because he'd missed family dinners for over a month now. The ongoing case he and his vice team were investigating kept him away from home. He was missing a lot more than just dinner.

A light murmur came from behind the living room door; he recognised Coronation Street's theme tune. Picturing his wife curled up on the sofa watching the evening soaps, he realised it had been a long time since they'd snuggled up together and enjoyed mindless TV. He walked deeper into the house, a thudding beat from Maggie's bedroom insulted his ears; he couldn't quite understand the noise teenagers called music these days.

Hamilton turned the kitchen light on and filled the kettle. It had been a manic day interviewing witnesses and all he wanted now was a warming cup of tea, a steaming hot shower and a good night's sleep.

"Your dinner's in the oven." Elizabeth surprised him from behind.

"I ate at the station."

His wife tutted as she retrieved the plate and scraped the unwanted food into the bin. "You would have! I don't know why I bother."

"Sorry, I should have called to let you know. But this case –"

"Blah, blah, blah! I've heard all about this bloody case and how busy you are, Denis. It always comes before us. It would be nice to be appreciated, or at least have someone notice I'm here. Maggie didn't touch a crumb of it either."

Hamilton abandoned what he was doing and gently wrapped his hands around Elizabeth's waist. He inhaled the fruity, flowery smell of Dior – of his wife – and was delighted when she didn't pull away from him.

"I'm sorry, I really am. As soon as this case is signed off I'm going to book some annual leave. The three of us should take a much needed holiday."

"Ha! You think that's the answer? More to the point, do you really think Maggie would come?"

"Of course she will. She's a good kid, Elizabeth, and we've always had fun when we go away together. We just need to get away from life for a bit, and it'll be a great way to celebrate the end of her exams. Besides, sixteen is not too bloody old to go on holiday with your parents. I would have jumped at the chance had my parents ever offered it to me. Mind you, that would have meant them actually spending time together as a couple."

Elizabeth stepped out of his embrace and frowned. "When is the last time you actually had a conversation with your daughter, Denis? She has no interest in anything anymore."

Hamilton shrugged, he couldn't remember the last time he'd seen Maggie for more than five minutes. He usually left for work before she was even awake, and was in bed by the time he came home.

"She's a teenager, Elizabeth! She's not interested in her parents but trust me, she'll jump at the mention of a week in the sun. How long has she been playing that noise?"

"A few hours. It's revision time and she's not to be disturbed."

"How can anyone revise for exams and have the music that loud?"

Elizabeth raised her hands in the air. "I have no idea, but I made the mistake of disturbing her the other day and got my head bitten off."

A look of sadness washed over his wife's face. Though her jet-black hair was neatly tied back and her make-up as fresh as when she applied it that morning, there was an emptiness in her emerald green eyes. She looked older than her thirty-three years. Guilt punched him in the stomach for deserting his family lately. He leaned forward and pecked her on the cheek.

"I'm sorry, darling. Let me have a chat with Maggie. Get her to turn the music down at least."

She smiled. "Good luck with that. I'll make the tea, shall I?"

As he climbed the stairs, Hamilton was cheerful that a fight hadn't erupted with Elizabeth. He was always on tenterhooks as to how his wife would react to his homecoming. But, it had pleasantly landed somewhere between awkwardness and a slanging match.

Perhaps some snuggling is on the cards.

He knocked on Maggie's door, but if she had responded he wouldn't have heard over Ed Sheeran blasting on repeat. He pushed open the door and froze. A gasp escaped, his heartbeat pounded like a drum. Maggie lay on the bed in her nightdress, her brunette hair spread around her, an empty litre bottle of vodka and a packet of pills next to her. He screamed for his wife and ran, skidding to the floor. He searched for a pulse, but her skin was ice-cold to touch.

Hamilton scooped his daughter up into his arms and, cradling her to his chest, buried his face in Maggie's hair. He ignored Elizabeth's screeches of panic and rocked back and forth; and, as the stereo sang *The A Team*, he finally heard the lyrics about angels flying.

CHAPTER THIRTEEN

Hamilton sensed the dark atmosphere the moment he opened his eyes. His wife, sat upright beside him in their dusky bedroom, sobbed uncontrollably. It didn't happen as often as it used too, but every now and then he would find Elizabeth in the depths of grief, and his heart would ache that little bit more. He switched on the bedside lamp, pulled himself up and wrapped his arms around her. Elizabeth fell onto him, her tears soaked his bare chest.

"It's okay, darling, I'm here. You're not alone," he whispered, and clung tighter to her slender frame.

No more words were needed; he'd discovered that in the weeks after Maggie's death. Somehow, he always managed to say the wrong thing and so, for half an hour they sat in the dimly-lit room in complete silence, before his wife lifted her head and looked at him. Her usual spellbinding green eyes were red and swollen, but she smiled through her evident pain.

"We'd better get ready or we'll both be late for work," Elizabeth said.

She pecked him on the cheek, slid out from under his arm and got up. Gazing in the mirror, Elizabeth attempted to control her bedhead hair by flattening it with her palms. Hamilton couldn't tear his eyes from her. Even after all these years, he loved to watch her, especially in the moments when she thought he wasn't looking.

"Maybe you should call in sick today," he said, breaking his own trance.

She walked to the end of the bed, placed her hand on her hip and rolled her eyes.

"But I'm not sick, Mr Hamilton." She pouted with a wink and he leapt from the bed to hug her. "Today is a bad day, but… the kids at school always help me through."

Certain it wasn't a dig, but hefty as a punch to the stomach nonetheless, he looked to the floor. "I'm sorry I haven't been around a lot lately… these cases…"

"Say no more, you know I understand." Elizabeth pulled away and waltzed off to their en-suite bathroom.

He sighed, knowing she needed the space to mentally prepare herself for the day, but it had left him feeling desolate. Sometimes they discussed a current investigation he was involved with, especially one that featured heavily in the media, but he couldn't bring himself to share the images of the dead children he had seen in the past few days.

"Maybe you could call Jacqui at The Red Lipstick Foundation," he suggested.

The charity had offered ongoing support to their family after Maggie's suicide, and Elizabeth had formed a special bond with their founder. Reluctant to ignore the heart-breaking scene just moments before, Hamilton felt compelled to comfort his wife. Elizabeth peered around the door and shouted over the gushing water from the shower behind her.

"I'm fine, Denis, honestly. Go on, off to work and catch the bad guys."

She winked before closing the door and, despite downplaying her sorrow, guilt gnawed away at Hamilton while he dressed for work. He glanced at his watch, conscious he was already running late. The team's intensifying investigation required all his time and energy, but he made a mental note to text Jacqui later and ask her to touch base with his wife. Elizabeth didn't return from the bathroom before Hamilton was ready to leave, so he shouted farewell through the door.

"Bye, Denis," she quietly replied. "Be careful out there."

When he finally arrived at the café, Fraser was already sitting at the table in the far corner. He stopped at the counter to buy a cup of tea, but the waitress explained it had already been ordered, and followed him over to the table. The pair waited while the grey-haired woman in a pristine, white apron set down their mugs and left. He couldn't remember the last time he'd requested a colleague meet him for a drink before their shift began, if indeed he ever had. Fraser fidgeted in her chair, twiddling strands of long blonde hair through her fingers.

"I thought it would be beneficial if we cleared the air, Kerry," he said, in an attempt to sound friendly.

"I have wanted to do the same myself, sir. I just wasn't sure how to go about it."

"You know my office door is always open," Hamilton replied, and she grimaced. "Well, usually it is. You have to understand, Kerry, I've worked in the Met for a long time. It's unfamiliar ground for me to have to explain myself, or my actions for that matter."

"I wasn't aware I had made you feel that way," she said, folding her arms.

"The tension in the office is palpable. You're a fantastic sergeant, but there will be times you have to work alone, and I expect you to follow orders without hesitation. Granted, it's bad timing, what with being without Wedlock and Morris –"

"I don't think that has anything to do with *this*," she interrupted.

His eyes roamed over her taut expression; it was clear this woman could not be fooled easily.

The instant Fraser had stepped into her interview less than six months ago, Hamilton sensed she was a strong character and filled with a desire to be on the team. He knew it wasn't fair to try and dupe her.

"Be frank, Kerry. What do you want me to say?"

The rain beat rhythmically against the misted windows like the second hand of a grandfather clock. Fraser made eye contact with her boss.

"I want to hear the truth. I spoke to DCI Allen and he said it was a conversation I needed to have with you. You were so supportive to me during our last murder investigation, and maybe it's because it was my first big case with you, but I just can't... I don't understand why you would shun away. Yes, I'm still the newbie, but you were so dismissive of me the other day."

"You're right. With the entire observation. I haven't been myself this week, not since the Paige Everett case, but I shouldn't have made you feel the way I have. There's a part of my life that I've learnt to block out, or at least push back from the surface, because it's the only way I can get on with everyday life."

Hamilton hesitated, took a few slurps from his now lukewarm tea and proceeded to tell Fraser about the night Maggie died. He spared no details, so she could fully understand the devastation scorched in his memory.

"I am so sorry, boss. I had no idea... no one told me."

He half smiled. "People at the station stopped talking about me, eventually. Those who know wouldn't dare mention it and those who don't? Well, that's because they don't need to."

"So... why are you telling me?"

"Despite the short service, you're a valued member of my team, Kerry. We have to trust each other, and you needed to know why I abandoned the Everett investigation. It wasn't because of you."

Her eyes widened. "The crime scene... it must have been a mirror image. The only difference being..."

"I know. It's not entirely the same situation, but Maggie was a victim of cyber bullying. I had no idea it was happening to her. She was taunted via Facebook and text messages while she was at home... the one place she should have felt safe. The place I should have made safe for her. But I was too busy to even notice."

The pair sat quietly as the momentum of customers picked up in the café; work men and uniformed officers rushed in for their takeaway bacon rolls and coffees. Hamilton's shoulders slumped. It was the first time he'd spoken so openly to someone other than Elizabeth about what had happened to their daughter. He had never forgiven himself and would take the guilt to his grave.

"I swore I'd never be like my father, that I'd always be there for my kids. The day Maggie died… I never felt more of a failure."

"You're not close then?"

"My parents had a rocky marriage and split when I was a teenager. My father returned to his family home in Jamaica and we never heard from him again. He never met Maggie." Hamilton paused, pushing away the outdated image of his father. "My mother? Now, she's a different story… she's amazing."

"Do you see her often?" Fraser asked.

"As much as possible, when you work in a demanding job like we do," he laughed. "She was born in London, grew up near here, and worked in St Thomas's Hospital for as long as I can remember. But when she retired, she moved to the Lake District, so I don't see her as often as I'd like to."

"What a lovely area of the country. You should make the time."

"She runs this quaint little tea room on the shore of Lake Windermere." Hamilton smiled and nodded. "Elizabeth and I will visit soon."

He felt at ease with his colleague, but then a lifetime of memories vied for his attention and his jaw tightened as the lump rose in his throat.

"Can I ask, what made you join the murder investigations team?" Fraser finally broke the silence.

"After Maggie's funeral, I was so angry I handed my notice in. My DCI at the time insisted I take compassionate leave, that we'd re-evaluate my decision at a later date. The grief threw Elizabeth and I together and, surprisingly, we grew stronger as husband and wife. In time, we found a way of waking up each morning, getting dressed and having breakfast without one of us falling apart. I turned my self-hatred into determination. I promised I'd do everything I could to stop miscreants walking these streets and help give their victims a voice… bring them justice. And no, Paige Everett is not the first teenage fatality since Maggie passed away, and sadly I know she won't be the last. But, everything about that crime scene… her Facebook on the laptop, the drug remnants on the desk, even her angelic pose on the bed. I could have been at home, in my daughter's room five years ago. It won't happen again."

"You don't have to explain to me, boss. I'm sorry you had to relive it, but it has shown me a different side to you. I don't know, maybe I understand you better and… well, thanks for that." She beamed the most genuine smile Hamilton had witnessed from a colleague. "You know it's been scientifically proven that sharing secrets with the people you work with is vital, especially if you're prone to volatile situations."

Hamilton laughed, her teasing infectious. "Well, maybe we'll have to get Clarke to join us, and you can both share your deepest and darkest secrets with the group."

"Hmm… no thanks, maybe not such a great idea after all. Heaven knows what that man is keeping buried. But feel free to reveal more about yourself, boss. I don't know anything about your wife."

"Don't push it, Fraser," he replied austerely, but couldn't hide the curve of his lip. "It's almost eight, let's get to the office. We finally have *someone* joining us today."

Hamilton took a note from his wallet and dropped it onto the table, signalling farewell to the waitress as they left the café.

"What's all that in there?" Hamilton pointed to the clear carrier-bag Fraser held.

She lifted it up for examination. He clearly spied the pint of milk, instant coffee and teabags. "Supplies for the office, because it's obvious no one else is going to replenish."

He nodded his head and grunted, only smirking once she had walked ahead of him. Normal service resumed, he thought, and hoped the new addition to the team wouldn't rock the now stable boat.

In the office, Hamilton identified the new sergeant immediately; as the only one wearing a T-Shirt and jeans combo, it wasn't hard. The man was much younger than he had expected, possibly late twenties, with a full head of dark hair and a short, lighter-coloured beard. He marched over, interrupting the punchline to Clarke's joke, and held out his hand.

"I'm DI Denis Hamilton, you must be Sergeant…"

The young man's cheeks flushed. "No, sir, I'm PC Robbie O'Connor. I've been transferred to help with your investigation."

"By whom?"

"DCI Allen made the request, sir."

Hamilton noted O'Connor's Irish accent and wondered if there was a family connection between the chief and new recruit. He raised an eyebrow questioningly.

"I mean he didn't personally request me," O'Connor continued, "but I'd heard there was a chance to work in London and I jumped at the opportunity."

"Where have you come from?"

"Welwyn, sir. I've been there three years but I'm looking to move to the city."

"This isn't a permanent position, lad. I'm waiting for a new sergeant to join the team. You're only here to cover compassionate leave."

O'Connor smiled, his white teeth shining as bright as his hazel eyes. "Understood loud and clear, sir. I'm just pleased to be part of the team, for however long that may be."

Hamilton wasn't impressed with the excited puppy-dog in front of him, but he could understand the lad's feelings. It was a big step for an aspiring sergeant and he had faith that O'Connor's request wouldn't have been granted if he didn't meet the standard.

"Okay, well we're going to have to throw you straight in at the deep end. I hope you're prepared for that, O'Connor."

"Of course, sir, one hundred per cent. And please, call me Rocky." Hamilton frowned, waiting for an explanation. "Well, what with the initials and the fact I do a bit of sparring in my spare time, this nickname was inevitable when I started my training in Hendon. Being called O'Connor by a colleague now seems a bit alien."

Hamilton wanted to remind the lad he wasn't a colleague, but a superior. Reminiscing over his time in uniform, the banter everyone shared and his own nickname of Ham, gratefully left behind, he nodded in agreement. As long as O'Connor was professional and efficient, he could be called whatever he wanted.

"Fine, Rocky, you'll be office-based with Fraser, for now at least. Get up to speed on our bedroom killer and then take your orders from her," Hamilton commanded. "We're in the process of trying to find a link between the two women."

"Boss, I've requested the victims' phone and bank records so we can cross-reference them," Fraser cut in. "Both their laptops are being delivered to me today, if they're not already in the building that is."

"Interesting, they could prove extremely useful."

"Well, I got to thinking, with the technology out there today, no one is truly a recluse. It's hard to stay anonymous during real-life support meetings and groups. But online…"

"You can be whoever you want and still find a wealth of help," Rocky finished Fraser's sentence.

"Exactly!"

Hamilton rubbed his hands together. "Well, it sounds like you two are on the same page already, great stuff. Fraser, utilise Rocky to get that side of the investigation moving along faster. An update from me about Tony Jones – husband of our second victim, Emma – he couldn't be located at his last known address, so hasn't been told about the murder yet. Clarke, we're going to head to his place of work and see if he's there."

"Find anything more about the restraining order, gov?" his partner asked.

"It was actually a non-molestation induction order Emma Jones had against him."

"So, we're talking the aggressive, possibly violent type of husband and father," Clarke replied. "Fraser, it might be worth seeing if our first victim had any connection to this Tony Jones. It's not unheard of for men to have secret wives and families."

"Really, just five miles apart?" Fraser questioned.

Clarke shrugged and replied mockingly, "Limits travel expenses."

"Actually, I think the idea may have legs," Hamilton said, for once agreeing with his partner's unfaithful way of thinking. "Consider all the possibilities and look into them. We're heading over to Camden now. Text me if you find out anything further on Jones in the next half an hour."

CHAPTER FOURTEEN

"We would have been better off getting the tube," Clarke exclaimed as he manoeuvred the car through the busy Camden High Street.

"You'd be on your own then, partner," Hamilton replied.

The thought of travelling on the London Underground, after so many years of driving, made his skin crawl. While it gave the opportunity to span huge distances of the city, without consideration for parking, the thought of standing nose-to-nose with a stranger filled Hamilton with dread. His arse pressed against the thigh of some man whose coffee-stained breath could warm his neck was out of the question. He'd choose the bustling roads of the city every time.

The pair had no choice but to park on a side street and walk five minutes back into the heart of Camden and over the lock. Despite the wet weather, shoppers were out in force for the famous market stalls, and pungent wafts of meats and spices filled their nostrils. He wasn't one to eat on the job, but Hamilton couldn't help but contemplate the thought of buying a kebab roll afterwards.

"This is the pub," Clarke said, and held the door open for him.

Hamilton marched through, staggered at the size of the crowd so soon after breakfast, and asked for Tony Jones.

"Who the bloody hell are you?" was the response given by a bald, six-foot man with the tattoo of a skull on his neck.

He knew they'd found their man and reached for his warrant card, unconcerned by those around him. "DI Hamilton and DS Clarke, we need a word please, sir."

Tony Jones flared his nostrils and clenched his jaw. Hamilton, ready to give chase, was surprised when the man lowered the empty pint glass to the counter and threw his head towards the side door. The pair followed Tony into a narrow corridor, allowing the noise of the pub to be sucked away through the vacuum of the door.

"What's this about? I ain't done nothing," Tony barked, as he stepped into an empty office.

"Take a seat please, sir. I'm afraid we have some bad news."

The man listened to Hamilton's instruction and sat silently while he imparted the painful information about Emma and Kyle Jones's murders. Tony appeared void of emotion, merely staring at the floor while running his forefinger over his thumb. Hamilton waited a few moments more, expecting a reaction.

"Mr Jones, is there someone you'd like us to call for you?"

"No, I… my…" he choked, and cleared his throat. "There's no one. Just… I can't fucking believe this."

Tony stood, walked to the other side of the office and rested his palms flat against the wall, hanging his head between them. Hamilton frowned at his partner, thinking it strange for the man to adopt a position they'd normally use to search a suspect.

"Where's the manager?" Hamilton asked, deciding to change tactics.

"He's out. Running errands."

"And you have permission to use his office?"

Tony spun around and frowned. "Yeah, he's a mate. Is that a problem?"

"I guess that's how you got this job. Must be difficult to catch a break when you have a criminal record."

"Are you for real? You've just fucking told me my wife and kid are dead, and you're giving me this shit!"

"Mr Jones, we know about the non-molestation order your wife had out against you."

"What, so I must have killed her? Screw you."

Hamilton watched closely as the man balled his hands into fists and aimlessly paced the room, his thoughts obviously elsewhere.

"When's the last time you saw your wife and son, Mr Jones?"

He relaxed his fists, rubbing one over his head. "I don't know, months ago, maybe. We'd split up. Her and Kyle lived somewhere else…"

"Then why the injunction order?"

"I don't know. She said I was following her, scaring her and the kid. I flaming wasn't."

"Mr Jones, there would have been proof to her claim."

Tony stopped walking and perched himself on the office table. "Okay, maybe when she first left I was fuming, but I only wanted to make her come back to me. I'd hang around places I thought she'd be, you know, the supermarket or hairdresser's or play centre. She took it all wrong, said I was stalking her."

Without the post-mortem results, Hamilton took a risk with the next question, using Audrey's unconfirmed estimation for the time of death. "Mr Jones, where were you two nights ago, in the early hours of the morning?"

"Probably here. You can check the rota, but I pretty much work every night shift because I live upstairs. Like I said, manager's a buddy."

"Explains why we couldn't find you earlier to inform you. Can anyone confirm they physically saw you?"

"Yeah, the bloody manager, he lives here too," Tony snapped. "Don't know if he'll be back tonight mind you."

"That's fine, we'll make sure your alibi is corroborated. What about your wife's family, we haven't been able to contact anyone else?"

"Nah, and you won't, I'm all she had really. Father ran away before she was born and her mother died last year. I'm telling you, it was as soon as that woman pegged it, Emma was hell-bent on leaving me. Was probably the old bag's dying wish."

"Did your wife have any enemies that you know of?" Hamilton continued, noting the frustrated tap of the man's right foot.

"How the hell would I know? I've been trying to get my life back on track after all the things she accused me of. I told you, I hadn't seen them and had no idea where they were living."

"Well, we will need to speak to you again at some stage, Mr Jones. So, you are not permitted to leave the area. Thank you for your time and sorry for your loss."

With his closing words, Tony finally met Hamilton's stare.

"Will I have to see them, you know all cut up and open?"

"Your wife and son were discovered by a friend and have been formally identified. However, as next of kin, we will ask the pathologist to contact you directly, and you will be entitled to see them both, Mr Jones."

"A friend? What fucking friend? Did she have another fella?"

"It was Lynn Bairden."

"That bitch knew where they lived… and I didn't?"

For the first time since meeting the man, Tony's eyes glistened for just a second before he roughly rubbed the tears away. Hamilton couldn't determine if it was due to the devastating news or the begrudging relationship, but he was adamant he would find out everything he could about Tony Jones.

CHAPTER FIFTEEN

Katy threw her head back and laughed at Frankie's transformer impersonation. Without understanding how, her son brought the sunshine out on a grey, cloudy day. Outside, the unseasonal rain had finally taken a break, leaving a light breeze and a glimmer of sunshine. The net curtains blew into the room and she drank in the fresh air. Craig had granted Katy's request for the weekend off work, and she was looking forward to spending some quality time with Frankie. Pushing her anxieties to the pit of her stomach, or at least ignoring them for a while, she was more determined than ever to enjoy herself. She wanted to abandon her fear and feel emancipated.

"Please come with us," Alexina had begged, before she, Lily and Nancy travelled to Sutton to visit their family. "My mother's garden is huge, the kids will love it, and I really don't think you should be here alone."

Grateful for Alexina's consideration, she decided against it. If Katy were to have any success making their new house a home, it needed to feel safe without running away at every hurdle. However, being the insistent type that she was, Alexina had given Katy a spare key to her flat, just in case.

Katy left her son to his robotic dance moves while she quickly loaded the washing machine. Checking each pocket of her jeans, she pulled out Matthew's card, and her stomach involuntarily flipped. Her fingertips roved over his name, and she wondered if she'd have the nerve to call him, or at least send him a text message. She shook her head, placed the card on the counter, and continued with her chores. There was just one more thing Katy needed to do.

"Frankie, I'll be ready shortly."

"Oh, Mummmmm! I thought we were going out," he called back.

"Give me twenty minutes and then I promise we can go into town for some ice-cream."

When no reply came, Katy seized the opportunity and switched on the laptop. At five years-old, her son had no concept of time – there was no telling if he'd give her ten minutes or an hour before the nagging began again. A quick glance at her inbox showed a few emails from Friends Online and her mind briefly wandered to Steven.

"Mummmmm," Frankie yelled from the living room, "that's been twenty minutes."

"More like two, darling. Watch one more Charlie and Lola and I'll be ready."

"Okay. I'm timing you."

Katy swiftly pulled opened another tab and entered a variety of keywords in the search bar. It was disappointingly difficult to purchase the products she'd had in mind, due to the strict laws in the UK. After some research, she discovered the legal alternative to the US Pepper Spray was a gel spray criminal identifier, which omitted a red gel and stained the attacker for at least a week. Fascinated by the self-defence spray, Katy ordered a twin-pack and a mini personal alarm. Just clicking the confirm button on the Amazon checkout filled her with a sense of power she hadn't embraced for many years.

Frankie, her small ball of energy, hopped from foot-to-foot at the front door as she slipped into her trainers. The stroll into town was peaceful, watching her son skipping a few paces ahead of her as she gazed around the empty streets, the large houses and surrounding greenery. Katy finally felt free, and erased the memory of Brad confronting her on the street. For once, her husband had listened and backed off, and she refused to spend any more time worrying about him.

She thought back to her old life, and London city, where the crowds of people fought for space on the pavements. They'd barge into each other, their attention focused on their mobiles, rather than the people they passed every day, and yet it was these mindless people and their gossiping nature that Katy worried about. While working at the salon, she'd heard too many tales about strangers and the dramas unfolding in their lives. The thought of becoming the centre of that hearsay, and receiving pity from clients and colleagues, made her feel violently sick.

The sun was breaking through the earlier dark clouds and she basked in the slither of sunshine, miles away from the fumes of her past, and ran to catch up with Frankie. Together they skipped the length of the high street, targeting Mario's, the Italian ice-cream parlour on the corner of the road. She had only brought her son here once before, not long after they'd moved to Hertfordshire, when he was missing home. Frankie had pestered her every week since to come back and now, seeing the smile beam across his angelic face, remorse attacked her for taking so long.

"Imagine bumping into you," a voice whispered behind her at the shop counter.

Katy turned and faced Matthew, his gaze hungrily trailed over her unstyled hair and make-up free face. She mumbled an excuse for the casual attire, and sighed internally at her lack of style.

"You must be Frankie," Matthew said, smiling down at the small person now clinging to Katy's leg.

"How did you know?"

"You told me, the other night in the pub."

Katy shrugged. "I guess we did speak a lot that night. What are you doing here?"

"I was out shopping and thought I spotted you. I love ice-cream, mind if I join you?" Matthew asked Frankie. "Add a strawberry milkshake and our bellies will turn into creamy volcanoes," he added, and exploded his hands into the air.

Frankie giggled, and finally released his grip on Katy. Matthew winked in her direction before walking along the length of the counter with her son. They discussed superheroes and desserts – adamant if they chose the green mint choc-chip they'd become the Hulk. She chuckled, a comment she'd never thought to say to her son, yet one that invited such amusement.

Katy ordered herself a coffee and took a seat at a table, watching the interaction between Matthew and Frankie. She thought of her own father and the close relationship she'd had with him. They had bonded over their love of literary characters, which hadn't been surprising, considering he was an English teacher. It was thanks to her father Katy had learned to understand and appreciate Shakespeare, and the tales he wrote. After her father's death, she threw all the classics away, a memory that now filled her with great regret. Brad swooping into her life was magical, and she had fallen for him as hard as Juliet had done for Romeo – if only their tragic ending had been a warning to her, she thought now.

"We've got our civil war going on," Matthew announced, as they rejoined her.

She eyed the mountains of cherry ice-cream in front of her son and the blue bubble-gum choice in Matthew's hand.

"Ah ha! Captain America versus Iron Man," she said, and crossed her fingers under the table.

Matthew tipped his head and casually saluted; a wave of relief flooded her. Katy suddenly knocked her cup, splashing the boiling liquid onto the table; she hated the effect he was having on her. Frankie picked up the complimentary colouring pad and crayons and busied himself.

"So, Matthew, I know you work in retail, but you didn't mention where."

"Next, in the Howard Centre. They snatched me away from the competition." He laughed. "I must have been doing something right, hey."

"Where did you work before?"

"John Lewis in Oxford Street."

"Oh, that's near where I used to work," Katy blurted.

"I specialise in marketing and promotions, so you wouldn't have seen me on the shop floor. It's more behind the scenes stuff."

"Are you finding it a big change from the bright, noisy city to this beautiful picturesque town?"

"Well, everyone asks far too many questions here, but I agree the scenery is lovely."

A mischievous expression spread across his face, and Katy continued to fumble with the wet tissues as she mopped the table, unable to keep eye contact with the handsome man.

"Mum, can I have another ice-cream? P-p-please?" Frankie interjected.

"No, sweetie. There really will be an eruption of some sorts if I let you eat any more."

He frowned. "Okay, can Matthew come back to our house? I want to show him my Bumblebee Transformer."

"Erm… well…"

"I'm sorry, buddy, I can't," Matthew interrupted her mumblings. "I've got plans tonight."

"Of course, yeah… so have we."

"Where are we going, Mummy?"

"It's home time, Frankie. Are you bringing those colours with you?" she asked, but didn't wait for an answer as she collected their belongings.

Matthew stood when she did, and lightly touched her hand. "But I *would* love to see you again. Both of you actually." Katy smiled, her heart beating as fast as a marathon runner's. "Look, I'm getting a taxi home now. I know you live near the pub, so I can drop you home first?"

"Yes please, Mum. My legs are too tired to walk *all* the way back home." Frankie stood between her and Matthew.

"Okay, sure, why not? Thank you."

"I'll call one. Meet you outside."

Katy slipped her son's coat on. He looked tired and she was pleased it was only a ten-minute drive home. The last thing she wanted was Frankie falling asleep too early; he'd be up again at midnight thinking it was midday. Once they joined Matthew outside, a pang of unexpected sadness swept over her at the thought of them going their separate ways shortly.

Conversation in the taxi was minimal. Katy wanted to ask Matthew about his plans, guessing he was off to a glamorous party where the women would be wearing sexy dresses that revealed just the right amount of cleavage, their hair expertly fashioned and make-up beautifully applied. The men would be in smart suits, circling the room and chatting about their successes, while the waiters would hover, serving canapés and champagne from silver trays in muted servility.

"Katy," Matthew said, pulling her from the daydream. "I meant what I said, about meeting up again, that is."

A giggle spontaneously escaped her lips and she nodded. "I'd like that too."

The car stopped and Frankie awkwardly clambered over Katy's lap to pull the door open. He shouted goodbye to Matthew and jumped out.

Matthew leaned in and gently pecked Katy on the cheek. "Hopefully I'll see you soon," he whispered, and looked over her shoulder out of the window. "Wait, is this where you live? I'm just on the other side of the park. It'll be quicker to just walk through than drive around the one-way system."

He reached into his pocket, took out a note and handed it to the driver, telling the man to keep the change. Frankie sped off through the communal front door and Katy cursed that yet again, it had been left unsecure on the latch. There was no other exit, but she hated the thought of her son alone, and a spark of realisation suddenly hit her.

"I'm sorry, Matthew, but I won't be able to see you again."

He flinched, as though she'd slapped him across the face. "I don't understand. I thought we had a good time."

"Oh, we did, I did. It's just... I need to focus on me and my son right now. I don't think it's the right time to get into anything like... well, like this."

Her hand gestured between them both and she smiled, hoping Matthew understood what she meant. Panic bubbled inside her stomach with Frankie out of sight, and the desire to bolt threatened to overwhelm her.

"That's fine. I mean, I'm disappointed of course, but I understand. Maybe when you're in a better place, give me a call," Matthew said, and waved goodbye.

Katy inhaled deeply, spun around and marched inside the building hoping he hadn't noticed her crimson cheeks. She wanted to glance back, wanted to know if he was still there, but instead she raced upstairs to find Frankie sitting cross-legged on the floor outside their home.

"I'm tired, Mummy."

"I know, sweetie. Early sleeps tonight I think."

While her son trudged into his bedroom, Katy carefully twisted and turned the keys, repeating the action three times until she was satisfied the door was locked; a security measure in her haste she had failed to complete downstairs.

CHAPTER SIXTEEN

After a briefing with his team, Hamilton stormed into his office and phoned the pathology lab. Another day with no convictions, or information from Audrey about the two crime scenes, caused his hands to shake. Patience was not a virtue he possessed when it came to murder. He waited, pen tapping against the desk, while the assistant placed him on hold. The pathologist was in a meeting, but he persisted and demanded to speak with the woman.

"Audrey Gibson –"

"It's DI Hamilton."

"Hello, Inspector. Say no more, I know why you're calling. Let me get my files together."

The line went quiet, but Hamilton could hear the rustling of papers and low humming. He didn't want to be the one to ruin the pathologist's mood, but he would if need be. This was not the time for merry singing.

"Ah ha, here it is. Sorry to keep you waiting, Inspector."

"Listen, Audrey," he said, faking a smile, hoping it softened his tone. "I fully appreciate how busy you are. I know you have many more cases on the go, other than mine, but I really need a forensic lead on the bedroom killings, so I can go out and catch this son of a bitch before he strikes again."

"And I thank you for your understanding, Inspector."

Hamilton noted Audrey's sarcastic tone, but ignored it when she sighed heavily and continued speaking.

"I was going to get in touch with you today. I apologise that you've had to make the call first, but this case isn't cut and dried, Inspector. Let me start by saying, both the male children died in the same manner; suffocation was determined from the pillows we found resting on their faces. There was no evidence of any other foul play, or injuries."

Hamilton couldn't disguise his relief, thanking God and rubbing his fingers against his temples. While still a horrific fate for all concerned, it was comforting to know the children hadn't suffered greatly.

"It's the female victims who held the attacker's interest," Audrey continued. "Please understand, the level of putrefaction that took place on the first victim's body made things much harder to establish. We have confirmed Scarlett Mitchell's identity by her dental records. I estimate time of death at approximately three weeks."

"One of your team members said it could have been up to a month ago, because of the missing fingernails?"

"Three weeks can also be enough time for the demise of fingernails, Inspector, which is exactly why I am always wary of giving information out at a crime scene. There's much to be considered, with this victim, factors such as age and weight, temperature and insects –"

"Okay, I understand," Hamilton interrupted, wincing at the thought of the Mitchell home and the smell of rotting eggs. "Continue with what you were saying before."

Audrey sighed. "The victim's organs had begun to burst, but not liquefy... those killed by asphyxia generally do decompose more rapidly. Both Scarlett Mitchell and Emma Jones suffered fractures to their hyoid bone which, considering its location in the neck is quite rare. Therefore, there is an indication that the amount of force inflicted was –"

"Are you saying they were both strangled?"

"It's easier to confirm with the second victim, given the speed at which her body was found, but yes, it's the cause of death I have reported for both cases. We also found a pubic hair in Scarlett's mouth; it was caught between the teeth so it was pulled from the root. We're running tests for a match. It's another marked difference from the second victim, Emma Jones, where there's no trace of hair transfer, but she had experienced deep vaginal injuries."

"Did you recover any sperm traces?"

"No. However, we did recover a piece of thread under her fingernail. Now, it doesn't match the top she was wearing, or the trousers on the floor, nor was there a match from the clothes her son was found in."

"So, it could be from the attacker. She could have fought back?"

"Possibly, Inspector, but it's a wool fibre. Woollen items are so widely available it would be impossible to pinpoint where it came from without having the original item to study. Gosh, it could be a hat or a jumper or –"

"A balaclava," he interrupted again, his train of thought now focused on the attacker.

"Yes, but that's indeterminate at this point. Give me something to work with. If you recover an item, I could match or discount it, but I can't guess its source. However, as we didn't find any unknown fingerprints, I have sent the wool off for analysis, along with the pubic hair."

"Okay, well at least this is something we can work on."

"You'll have to give me at least a week for the DNA results, Inspector, but I will call you the moment they're in. I want you to catch this monster too."

As though the woman on the other end of the line could see him, Hamilton raised a hand in surrender. "I know, of course you do and thanks, Audrey. A match is vital information to this case, so I'll wait patiently. Well, I'll try at least."

"A watched phone never rings, Inspector," she said with a giggle, and ended the call.

He told Clarke to follow him as he marched back through the office, out of the building and into his car. During the short drive to Pimlico, he updated his partner about the pathology report and explained the need to revisit the first crime scene. The victim's laptop was in Fraser's possession, and a full inspection had been carried out by the crime scene investigators, but Hamilton wanted to get a feel for who this woman was – what type of a person was she, and how she lived her life? Was there something of significance in her home that could tell him something about the attacker?

The putrid smell still overpowered the small flat. Hamilton and Clarke used their tops to cover the odour, pulling them high over their noses so their hands were free to roam.

"An initial door-to-door investigation took place, didn't it? Hamilton mumbled through the material of his jumper."

"Yes, but not much is useful information. Scarlett Mitchell only lived here for six months and no one really knew her." He stopped to flick through his notes. "The only thing that caught my eye from the files was the elderly neighbour across the hall. She was adamant a man entered the flat late one night, maybe a few weeks ago, but she couldn't be sure."

"What, that's the only information uniform took from her?"

"Yeah, pretty much. A tad shoddy if you ask me."

"There should have at least been a follow-up! I'll be sure to find out who took the original statement from the neighbour and give them a bloody good talking to."

Hamilton groaned, and made a mental note to drop in on the witness before they left. He asked Clarke to tackle the two bedrooms while he strolled around the open-plan kitchen and living room, eyeing every wall hanging, photograph and fridge magnet. There was a huge difference between this home and that of the second victim's, Emma Jones… for a start it was homely. There was a collection of home-made drawings clipped onto the fridge and dust clung to the many frames around the room. Hamilton collected a photograph of Scarlett, her son and an unidentified man. The Mitchells may not have lived here long, but there were personal possessions everywhere. With the foundations of a full life in this home, he speculated as to why no one knew the woman.

The shrill squeal of a passing train's wheels against the metal tracks made the hairs on Hamilton's neck stand to attention. He slowly turned in a circle, and although his eyes drifted over everything in sight, he couldn't shake the feeling he was missing something. Clarke burst into the room wafting a piece of paper in the air.

"Check this out, gov. A death certificate for a Mr Fred Crawford."

Hamilton peered at the photograph he still held. "I wonder if that's this guy," he said, and the two men exchanged potential evidence. "Hmm, well it's clear this man didn't die of natural causes... traumatic injuries to the abdomen it says here."

"It was in our victim's bedside cabinet. Bit bare in there really, just a few of Scarlett's clothes and women's bits. It was definitely just her and the kid living here."

"Call the team and have Fraser or Rocky find out who this Fred Crawford is. I want full details by the time we're back in the office. Tell them we'll bring lunch with us."

Hamilton returned the certificate to his partner and left the room. He had a quick look in the bathroom and hallway cupboard, but saw nothing of interest. He hovered outside the child's bedroom and took a deep breath before stepping inside. Losing a child was an unexplainable and gut-wrenching ache, and Hamilton couldn't decide if it was comforting to know Scarlett Mitchell would never feel the pain he did.

"Everything done, gov. Fraser is on the case with our mystery man," Clarke interrupted his thoughts.

"Okay. I don't think we're going to find anything in here," he said, scanning the room of Roald Dahl books and Lego sets. "Let's pop in on the neighbour before we head back."

After waiting what felt like a full five minutes, Karen Taylor finally opened her front door. Clearly a frail woman, stooped over with the aid of a walking stick, she wore her white hair in a tiny pony-tail at the top of her head. Once the introductions were made, she slowly led Hamilton and Clarke into her living room.

If he had thought the victim's home was filled with personal possessions, Karen's collection trumped that. Books, photographs and ornaments were crammed on shelves, above the fireplace and in an oak glass cabinet. An identical cabinet filled the opposite wall and was adorned with at least a hundred thimbles of different colours and designs. The coffee table was piled high with an assortment of magazines and, although there was a mountain of belongings, it looked clean and welcoming.

"Can I get you gentlemen a drink?"

"No thank you, Ms Taylor."

"Oh, please call me Karen," she said, slowly lowering herself down into the beige armchair covered in a flowery design.

Hamilton and Clarke sat on a miss-matched burgundy sofa on the other side of the room. His arse fell into the soft cushion a lot further than he was expecting, and he adjusted himself, sitting forward on the edge.

"Karen, we wanted to ask you a few questions about your neighbour, Scarlett Mitchell."

"I told the young black girl, the one in the uniform who was here when they found the bodies… those two poor souls...." She made the sign of the cross over her chest and reached forward to grab a packet of cigarettes.

Hamilton thought of the attending officer he had spoken to briefly when he had arrived at the scene. He understood, only too well, how she must have felt that day, but it didn't excuse the lack of detail in the statement. He decided a quiet word with the officer, a friendly warning not to mess up in future, would suffice as a one-off.

"We know you did, Karen, but we just need to clarify a few things," he continued. She lit a cigarette and eased back into the chair, her body visibly relaxing with the nicotine fix it received. "You told our officer you saw a man entering Scarlett Mitchell's home. Can you remember when it was you saw him?"

"Not really, we're talking weeks, dear. It was very early in the morning, and I only noticed because I had got up to use the toilet and heard something outside. I don't usually like to pry, but as I was in the hallway anyway, I had a quick peek through the spyhole."

"Did you manage to see what he looked like, or what he was wearing?"

"No. My door is directly opposite so I only saw the back of him. He was tall and had the hood of his coat up. I did think it strange he was wearing gloves but then, who knows how cold it gets in the early hours of the morning? I hardly ever venture out and I'm not one to judge."

"And what about Miss Mitchell? Did you hear anything she said?"

"She wasn't there, dear. We might seem on top of each other in this block, but it's a solid building. I can't hear through walls."

"What do you mean she wasn't there, Karen? Did Miss Mitchell open the door?" Hamilton shifted closer to her, listening intently as she exhaled another puff of smoke into the already misty room.

"No, the man had a set of keys. It was the noise of them jangling together that made me look. I assumed she'd found herself a nice boyfriend."

CHAPTER SEVENTEEN

The incident room was at its usual height of business as Hamilton joined his team. Rocky had comfortably taken over Wedlock's workstation next to Fraser, and looked much smarter now he'd changed into a shirt. Hamilton thought of his old colleague and wondered how the sergeant's mother was recovering; he vowed to call Les and check in when things were less hectic.

Their evidence board conveyed more details than when he had left; images of Tony Jones and Fred Crawford had been added. Crawford looked younger here than in the photograph from Scarlett's apartment, and the non-smiling pose signified a classic driving licence shot.

"Looks like you have an update for us, Fraser," Hamilton said purely out of habit, but immediately regretted ignoring Rocky. The lad may only be here as a pair of helping hands, but it was clear Rocky wanted to climb the ranks, otherwise why would he have volunteered for the role? "Let me bring you up to speed with what we've discovered from Audrey and our visit to Scarlett Mitchell's house."

Clarke used the time to make a much needed round of teas and coffees, re-joining them at the exact moment Hamilton opened the floor for information from Fraser and Rocky.

"I was looking into the two female victims, sir," she explained. "Frustratingly, I'm still waiting for their financial information; I'll chase that up as soon as we're finished here. But, from what I've uncovered from their laptops, both women were users of online dating or friendship websites."

Hamilton leaned against the wall, his fingers wrapped around the hot mug as Clarke perched on the table between Fraser and Rocky. No one interrupted her.

"From what I can ascertain, they were not members of the same website, and they did use their real names. I'm combing through the list of people they both interacted with to see if I can find an overlap. This information prompted me to look deeper into their social media activity and, in the last year, neither Scarlett or Emma communicated with anyone this way."

Clarke shook his head. "No way! They were both in their early thirties. You're telling me they weren't using Facebook, or Twitter, or even Instagram, never sharing pictures of their kids?"

"Contrary to what you may believe, not everyone enjoys publicising every single detail about their lives," Fraser retorted. "We've already established they were lonely women, and if someone truly wants to remain undetected, ignoring social media is a great start. However, they both had semi-active email accounts. Scarlett was in conversation with local schools about enrolment and Emma chatted with her friend, Lynn, and searched for part-time jobs; but, what I can't find is anything to suggest she was invited for an interview."

"Okay, well the online websites are a good connection to start with," Hamilton finally said. "Make that your top priority for now, but I want to know as soon as you have some financial information. What were these women doing for an income?"

His team nodded in agreement, but added nothing further, obviously feeling as irritated as he did. Sometimes, sieving through the mud of insignificant details could be just as difficult as working on a case with no evidence at all. Hamilton felt they were all being pulled in different directions of thought and, for the time-being at least, he couldn't envisage there being any resolve.

"What about our mystery man?" he asked.

"That's my cue then," Rocky replied.

There was an air of confidence about the newest member of the team; a quiet cockiness that could also be construed as eagerness, and therefore a likeable quality in Hamilton's book. He hoped it would stay at this level, and the secondment would not create a complete arsehole of Rocky – he'd worked with plenty enough of those in his time.

"Okay, Rocky, what do we know?"

"Fred Crawford was murdered nine months ago, in Luton, stabbed in the abdomen and died before arriving at the hospital. He disturbed a teenager mugging an elderly lady and received the fatal blow for his efforts."

"You see, this is why members of the public are so reluctant to get involved and help the community," Clarke exclaimed. "You never know when it's a sad case of wrong place, wrong time."

Hamilton straightened up and placed his empty mug on the desk. "How does this connect to our victim?"

"Crawford was Scarlett Mitchell's fiancé and Kyle's father, sir," Rocky continued. "I rang around and managed to have a quick chat with one of the officers involved with Crawford's murder case. He told me the man died in Scarlett's arms in the middle of the road; she was obviously distraught. The robbing teenager was arrested soon after and convicted. I was also able to get a previous address for Scarlett Mitchell."

"Well done, Rocky," Hamilton said, and turned to examine the evidence board. "I like the headway we're making with the victims, but it's the killer…"

His eyes roamed over the crime scene photographs, taking in the physical positioning of the half-naked victims, and the lack of obvious disruption to the homes.

"Both Scarlett and Emma were assaulted and attacked on their beds. It's personal and intimate," Fraser called over his shoulder.

Clarke stood and walked closer to the board, then turned to face them. "They're also lying on their backs, which could suggest our attacker wanted the women to watch what he was doing to them."

"So perhaps the fibre isn't from a balaclava," Fraser replied.

Rocky grumbled. "It still could be... he wore it so they wouldn't recognise him, but my guess is, it's more about him having power over them, and watching the fear he generates."

"Unfortunately, it doesn't matter if they recognised him or not," Hamilton said. "But I agree with Rocky about the attacker's controlling trait. Look at the photos, there's no gags or bindings restricting the women. He could be physically overpowering them and didn't need restraints, or he's used the women's desire to protect their children against them. Perhaps he promised not to harm their sons if they didn't struggle."

"I think we'd be crazy to ignore the mysterious man entering Scarlett's house... he had keys," Clarke said. "And we could say the same for Emma's apartment, as there was no forced entry."

"So, our attacker either knew the women, or was at least close enough to them to steal their keys?" Fraser's question hung in the air.

Hamilton contemplated whether the connection was purely the fact these women were lonely, single mothers. He finally pulled his eyes away from the evidence and addressed his team.

"We've uncovered nothing to make us think the sons were the targets, so it's vital we find a stronger link between these female victims. Fraser and Rocky, I want you to head over to the previous address we have for Scarlett Mitchell. Speak to the neighbours and find any friends she might have had. Let's see if we can build up a picture of this woman, and why she fell under the radar six months ago."

Rocky glanced at his watch. "Sir, do you mind if I go straight home from there? It's not a bad drive from Luton to Welwyn, but to detour back through London would be a mission."

"That's where you live, mate, Welwyn?" Clarke asked.

"At the moment, I do. I'm in the middle of a messy divorce. A friend of mine has been putting me up for a few weeks, but the ex wants all my stuff out of the house by tonight. It's just another reason why I want to find a place in London."

Hamilton smiled at Rocky, surprised by the lad's revelation. He really hadn't pegged Rocky as the married type, and wondered whether his judgement skills might be on the decline.

"How old are you, Rocky?" he enquired.

"Twenty-eight, sir." He grinned, and casually rubbed his fingers over his neatly trimmed stubble. "I know, my youthful looks probably fooled you. They do everyone."

Hamilton rolled his eyes, but grunted a laugh. He couldn't help it, the lad brought a freshness with him. Banter existed in the team, it needed to with the horrors they saw on a daily basis, but there was something about Rocky. Something Hamilton found engaging.

The office phone shrilled and they waited in silence while Clarke took the call, grunting and raising his eyebrows to gain their interest.

"That was one of the officers who attended the crime scene with us," Clarke informed them after he'd ended the call. "You'll never guess who's downstairs in custody for aggravated assault… Tony Jones. They've asked if you want to go down and have a chat with the arresting officer."

Hamilton frowned. "Yeah, I bloody well do. I want to know what's going on. Okay, Rocky and Fraser head home after your interview – I want a full investigation on the neighbourhood, noting absolutely anything of interest. I'll check this out and we'll reconvene for a briefing at eight in the morning."

CHAPTER EIGHTEEN

Sleep evaded Katy as it always did. Her mind crammed with images of Brad and Matthew and then Alexina; overwhelming anxieties of how quickly her life had changed again in just a few months. Resigned to the fact she couldn't relax, Katy got up, and ensured the keys were still hanging in the lock, and the door was secure. In the bathroom, she shed her clothes, keeping the light switched off so the noise of the extractor fan wouldn't wake her son. Led by the moonlight shining through the frosted-glass window, she stood in the bath and turned the shower on.

The hot water poured over Katy's porcelain skin. She closed her eyes, and rolled her head from side to side, the neck muscles clicking in protest of the stretch. A gentle touch caressed the back of her thigh. She jumped, clinging frantically to the window ledge for support and spun around. The fallen sponge sat innocently in the bath soaking up the water, and her quickening heartbeat returned to a steady pace. Katy routinely washed, turned the water off and climbed back out of the bath. The apartment was cloaked in stillness again.

Katy wrapped herself in a towel and hurried along the hallway to her bedroom. Pulling a fresh T-shirt over her head, she froze mid-action at the unmistakable sound of a glass bottle connecting with the kitchen tiles. Her feet refused to move. Her hands trembled as she lowered the material over her body, standing rigid while silently listening. The squeak of the floorboard echoed through her silent home. The crunch of leather deafening.

She tip-toed to the side of her bed and retrieved the baseball bat from its usual position behind the headboard. With a blank mind, her robotic and automatic actions urged her forward. Katy crept towards her bedroom door with the weapon clutched in her clammy hands. Another squeak. Deep breathing, so alien from her own, came from somewhere nearby. Katy desperately wanted to switch a light on, to convince herself she was over-reacting. But she knew that was a lie.

Her heartbeat raged in protest as she slid along the wall into the hallway, catching the whiff of a familiar aftershave. Katy took a small step, glided out into the middle of the landing and turned the corner. There he stood, towering over her and staring into her eyes. She shrieked, dropping the bat as she tried to get away. His hand reached for her bare neck.

He tightened his grip and she struggled for air. Katy thought of her son. She thrust her knee into his groin with such force, he released his hold and tumbled to the floor. She grabbed the baseball bat and sprinted past the intruder into her son's room.

"Frankie! Frankie!" she screamed, tearing the duvet from his tiny body. "Get up, we have to leave."

As much as she didn't want to scare him, panic gripped her. The aggressive moans from the other side of the door increased in their intensity. Frankie mumbled as Katy grabbed his shoulders and shook him.

"Frankie, follow me. If mummy tells you to run just do it, and don't look back."

Her son blinked and opened his eyes at the urgency in her voice. He opened his mouth, but Katy sealed it with her finger and shook her head.

She reached out her left hand and took Frankie's, keeping him tucked behind her as they walked out of his bedroom. The intruder was knelt on one knee, and pulled himself up with the support of the wall. Instinctively, she dropped her son's hand, wrapped both of hers around the bat handle and swung it into the side of the man's head. Frankie screamed.

The intruder slumped back and Katy threw the weapon down. Sweeping Frankie up into her arms, they jumped over the body. She unlocked the front door, yanked it closed behind her and locked it again from the outside. Halfway up the stairs she remembered Alexina wasn't home, and raced down the three flights of stairs. Wrapped around her hip, Frankie sobbed as Katy ran out into the shadowy street barefoot and frightened.

Scanning the deserted street, she frantically tried to formulate a plan. It was after midnight when she'd had a shower, and they'd escaped the apartment without a penny. Her eyes darted to the three-storey house across the road. Samantha. Katy took flight again. With her hand shielding Frankie's head, she pressed him further into her shoulder. She banged on the front door, shouting the babysitter's name, while desperately looking over her shoulder to watch the entrance of her own apartment.

A light shone behind the glass panels of the front door and a silhouette grew closer to open it. Jolene, Samantha's mother, peered out wearing a fluffy, cerise dressing gown and a large, pink hair roller in her fringe. Katy tore past the woman, pushing through her into the house and slammed the door shut.

"Call the police," she demanded.

"What the hell are you doing?" Jolene replied, wrapping the thick cotton material closer around her chest. "You can't just –"

"I'm sorry," Katy panted. "I've just been attacked in my home. *Please* call the police."

Jolene studied her and then Frankie. She couldn't be sure if Jolene recognised them, but Katy didn't have the strength to explain. Tears furiously rushed to meet her eyelashes as her body crumpled. Jolene managed to catch her arm and whisked them both into the nearby kitchen.

"Stay here," the woman said. "I'll call the police immediately." As Jolene walked out of the room, she stopped and turned to face them. Frankie sat on Katy's lap in a foetal position, his head buried into her chest. "Then I'll get you some blankets and make a hot drink."

Jolene left the room and Katy cradled her son, made nervous by the unfamiliar surroundings. She couldn't concentrate; the masked face and her husband's wild eyes were all that filled her mind. Thirty minutes later, Samantha had joined them and taken a reluctant Frankie into the living room. PC Lakhani arrived and sat opposite Katy with a female officer whose introduction she'd immediately forgotten. He asked her to relive the last hour, explaining what had happened.

"It's him! It's Brad," Katy screamed. "I told you he had found me. I told you he would hurt me again."

"Mrs Royal, we were unable to find your husband," PC Lakhani said.

"What?" Katy threw her hands in the air.

"At the station, after you gave me your statement, I made initial enquiries. Your husband wasn't at his home or work address."

"And that's it? You didn't think to warn me? He's obviously been stalking me this entire time and you've done nothing!"

Katy's rage bubbled through her veins. She jumped down from the breakfast bar and paced the enormous kitchen, running her hands through her hair.

"Mrs Royal," PC Lakhani continued, "we have officers and forensics in your apartment at this very moment."

"Well, at least you can arrest him now." She released a loud sigh, stopped walking and looked at the officers. The frown etched on the man's face was not a welcoming one. "What?"

He cleared his throat. "There's no one in your home. The forensic team have found a trail of blood, but there's no body."

Katy's body failed her again. The officer's words echoing over and over in her mind. She reached out for the chair but it was too late, and she fell to the floor. Colours blurred past her as muffled voices filled the air. Unidentifiable noises screeched in her fragile ears.

"Mrs Royal? Mrs Royal? I think we need the paramedics in here."

"No," Katy slurred.

Jolene returned to the kitchen and crouched in front of her, smiling and whispering something she couldn't understand. The two officers beside Katy helped her into a sitting position.

"I'm fine," she said, but PC Lakhani and his colleague supported her regardless. Katy shook them off and sat back at the breakfast bar. "I said I'm fine."

"Mrs Royal, it might be worth getting checked out at the hospital –"

"No! No. I need to think."

"You're suffering from shock –"

"How could he not be in the apartment?" Katy interrupted the officer again. "I locked the front door behind me. I bloody locked him in."

"The front door was still locked when we arrived. Did your husband have a key?"

Katy's head wobbled from side to side. "Only I have a key to my home. Besides, when I'm at home I always leave my keys in the front door. Even if he had a key, he wouldn't be able to open it with them inside."

"It's the back door that was opened, Mrs Royal. He escaped via the balcony, and then the communal door you share with your neighbour."

Katy gasped. "There was no key in that door…" her voice trailed off, realising the error she'd made.

"Mrs Royal… Mrs Royal?" The officer's calls finally dragged Katy back from her thoughts. "We will need to take an official statement from you. Is there somewhere you can stay tonight?"

"Katy and Frankie can stay here," Jolene answered.

As thankful as she was for her neighbour's kind gesture, bile rose in Katy's throat at the thought of being so close to where she'd been attacked. Brad would be waiting somewhere out there in the dark. He'd want his revenge for her overpowering him once more.

"Thank you, Jolene, but I can't stay here," Katy replied, and zoned out. She stared at the white kitchen tiles, the assault replaying like a film in her head.

PC Lakhani lightly touched Katy's shoulder to get her attention. She looked at his face; the sun-tanned skin and warm, brown eyes soon disappeared in a haze as her tears returned. It was stupid of her to think she could make a home for herself away from Brad. He had proven, once more, he could find her. She had fought against him too many times and feared for her life. Her husband had come to kill her tonight. Of that she was sure.

"Mrs Royal, I want to take you to the hospital. Just for a quick check over and then we'll make sure you get to wherever you want to go. You do have somewhere else to stay, don't you?"

Katy thought for a moment before nodding. "Yes, my aunty. Well, an old friend of my parents, but she's practically family… Wait, I need my bag! A Nike backpack, it's in the bottom of my wardrobe. It just has some clothes for me and Frankie, and some money."

"Okay, I'll see if we can grab that for you before we head off to the hospital," PC Lakhani said, and exited the kitchen.

Jolene came over and draped her arms around Katy, hushing her as they rocked back and forth. The unexpected gesture left Katy feeling uncomfortable, but thought it too impolite to shrug off the woman who had just been dragged out of her nice warm bed, and straight into a nightmare. She'd give Jolene a few minutes more, but then she had to get her son and escape. The stifling air attacked her like a winter fog.

The next hour raced by in a dark mist. Katy and Frankie clung to each other as they were transported from house to police car to hospital ward. The intrusive sharp lighting kept her from resting, even as her exhausted body sat motionless. Despite the clattering of equipment, screams from other patients and machine beeps, Frankie slept soundly on her lap. He refused to move away from his mother.

She always thought it strange how hospitals filled people with dread. It was easy to associate them with death and pain, but Katy felt safe. She hadn't watched her parents slowly die, attached to machines while they fought for their last breath. They had left their home to see a theatre show, and she'd waved them off as the car pulled out of the driveway. An hour later their bodies were in a mortuary. Their car written off, because another driver had sent a text message while driving. Instead, she thought about the day Frankie was born, in a hospital very similar to the one they were in now, and she hugged him a little tighter.

PC Lakhani entered the ward with a young nurse, the dark circles under her eyes suggesting this wasn't her first night shift of the week. They requested Katy follow them into a private cubicle. Frankie stirred as she stood up and readjusted him. His legs automatically wrapped themselves around her waist, and she slung the Nike bag over her other shoulder. She followed the official pair a few paces behind, allowing them to chat; she was sure PC Lakhani was flirting. She smiled and looked away, peering through the widows of the different wards they walked past. Katy halted, a low shuddering noise escaped her lips and PC Lakhani rushed to her side.

"What's wrong, Mrs Royal?" he asked.

Her body was weak, but she pointed to the patient on the other side of the window. The officer followed her gaze to a man lying on the bed, his eyes closed and a bandage covering the top of his head.

"That's him. That's my husband. That's Brad," she whispered.

Without waiting for a reply from the officer, Katy ran back the way they had come, her arms squeezing Frankie to her. She charged into people, hearing the insults shouted in her wake, but Katy paid them no attention. The determination to put as much distance between her and Brad overpowered everything. She couldn't remember running so fast in her life. PC Lakhani's voice echoed in the distance, roaring her name through the corridors. She was furious. Why was he following her when he should be arresting that monster of a husband? Frankie's cries triumphed over all other noises and spurred her on towards the automatic doors ahead.

Katy ran out into the middle of the night for a second time. The headlights from streaming cars and ambulances momentarily blinded her. Shielding her eyes with one hand, she strained to see out into the distance. She leapt in delight when she spotted a friendly face and raced off again. Clambering into the car, and with Frankie gripping her neck, she relaxed back onto the cushioned seat. Driving past the hospital entrance, she watched PC Lakhani end his chase.

CHAPTER NINETEEN

Hamilton was the first person in the office, and half an hour earlier than they had planned to convene. He enjoyed the morning peace, although it didn't come often in the incident room, and drank a strong mug of tea while examining the evidence boards again. Photographs, area maps and lists of personal belongings glared back at him, all vying for a connection to be made. The connection was there, he knew it was, but its elusiveness frustrated him.

As the team began to join him, Hamilton noticed Rocky was late. His annoyance grew. DCI Allen had relinquished some of the tasks and research to other detectives in the office as it became clear more assistance was needed on the case. But, as a point of rule, he would not stand for anything less than one-hundred per cent effort from his own team.

"Right, I'm not hanging around this morning, it's gone eight a.m. and we need to crack on. Fraser, can you give us an update on what you and Rocky discovered yesterday at Scarlett Mitchell's former address?"

She gazed at her watch before making eye contact with her boss. It was only five minutes after eight, and he reckoned Fraser probably thought he'd been a bit tough, but right now Hamilton couldn't care less. The bodies of two mothers and their sons had been discovered, he didn't want another family to meet the same fate because of his team's lack of punctuality.

"Sadly, not much, boss," Fraser answered. "It seems she and Fred were a quiet couple. They were new parents who didn't socialise too much with anyone in the area. Her closest neighbour did tell us that after Fred's murder she tried to reach out to Scarlett, to offer support, but it was unwanted. She said Scarlett fell into a state of depression and within a matter of weeks there was a 'for sale' sign outside the house. The neighbour never saw Scarlett or her son again."

"That's not very helpful," Clarke grunted.

"Well, how many of your neighbours are you friends with?" Fraser retorted, and he shrugged. "Because none of my neighbours really know me, or what I do for a living. It's human nature these days to keep yourself to yourself."

Clarke groaned. "I guess you're right. So, do we think her fiancé's murder has anything to do with this case, or is it just a coincidence?"

"Well, we can't ignore it," Hamilton said. "If anything, it could be the reason she moved to another area, took to hiding in her own apartment and ultimately was left alone. Similar to Emma Jones, whose husband was the reason she kept a low profile."

"Did you find out why he was arrested last night, gov?"

"Yes, it would seem Tony Jones had a night off from work and decided he wanted to be on the other side of the bar. He got drunk and got involved in a fight with his boss."

"I thought they were 'buddies'," Clarke mocked.

Hamilton grunted. "That's alcohol for you. And the man obviously has a temperamental personality."

"Still, I don't think he's involved in his wife's murder. Okay, he's not a nice character, but I don't know, he…" Clarke trailed off as Rocky opened the door and floated through the office, a grin plastered over his face.

"Again, let's not ignore Tony Jones. He remains a person of interest, especially until we've heard back from Audrey about any possible DNA," Hamilton continued, refusing to acknowledge the young police officer.

Rocky dropped the smile and cleared his throat. "I'm really sorry I'm late, sir."

"It's not a trait I let fly in my team." Hamilton's tone was harsh, but he gestured for Rocky to take a seat and join them.

"Of course not, sir, I totally understand. But I have some news that I think is beneficial to the case."

Hamilton rolled his eyes. "Well, don't leave us all in suspense. Spill…"

"Right, after our trip to Luton last night," he paused and looked at Fraser. "Have you updated them about that?" She nodded in reply. "Okay… so I went home. Well, not home obviously, but over to my ex-missus to collect my stuff –"

"Rocky, we know all this already. Do you think you could get to the interesting bit?" Clarke cut in.

Hamilton unexpectedly felt sorry for the new recruit. The lad was there to help and to learn, but it appeared his team were shunning Rocky's enthusiasm.

"I'll cut a long story short; when I was leaving for work this morning, my flatmate was coming home. He told me about a scene he attended last night. You see, he should have been home hours earlier, but the victim had taken flight."

"You share a flat with another officer?" Hamilton asked.

"Yes, sir. PC Lakhani and I work at Welwyn station."

He contemplated asking why this PC had no nickname like Rocky, but, worried it would launch him into another tale they didn't have time for, he bit his tongue and waved Rocky's story on.

"The victim, Katy Royal, was attacked in her home last night. But here's the real kicker, and there's actually more than one – Katy is a single mother to a young boy and the intruder was wearing a balaclava."

"She survived?" Hamilton confirmed, now extremely interested.

"Yes, sir. She's adamant it was her husband who she ran away from a few months previously because of domestic abuse. PC Lakhani filed her report on him a few days before the attack." Rocky continued to bring his colleagues up to speed on the events that led to Katy running from the hospital. "However, Lakhani couldn't find her outside so he went back into the hospital. It turns out Brad Royal was admitted days before, after being attacked and left for dead on the road. There's no way he could have attacked her last night."

"Hang on," Clarke said. "I understand the similarities, but the two other victims lived so close together. Now our murderer just ups and travels at least an hour's drive from Central London to Welwyn in Hertfordshire?"

"Well, if you let me finish," Rocky jested, making the rest of the team chuckle.

Hamilton couldn't determine if it was the excitement they all felt about a potential new lead, or if in fact Rocky's personality was growing on them, but they suddenly hung on the officer's every word.

"Katy Royal has connections to Central London. She lived here before running away to Welwyn, and said there was an aunt still living here and she would stay with her."

"Has the Welwyn station followed it up?" Hamilton enquired.

"No, sir. Lakhani drove by her apartment last night, thinking she may have returned after the hospital, but it was empty. Katy only mentioned the woman once, and gave no name or address."

Hamilton took a minute to process the information. They had a surviving witness to what seemed like a connected case. They had to get her into the station and take a statement from her. It also troubled him that, if the attacker was not the woman's husband, she may well be a vulnerable target.

"Okay, here's what's going to happen," Hamilton said. "I'm going to update the Chief and inform him we'll need to work with the Welwyn station. Fraser, I want everything you can find on Katy Royal and if she has absolutely any connection with the other two victims. Rocky, find this aunt! It's imperative we find Katy, so get me an address. Clarke, go and get the car ready. We're taking a drive to Welwyn."

As instructed, his partner raced from the room. Hamilton grabbed the phone to make a call to DCI Allen, but his fingers lingered for a moment over the buttons. He looked over to Rocky who was already drumming passwords into the keyboard.

"That is okay with you, isn't it Rocky? Clarke and I handling the interview in Welwyn? I mean, it is your turf," Hamilton called out.

The lad's face flushed a deep crimson, but his smile took over. "Of course, sir. It's exactly what I would have expected to happen... but I totally appreciate you asking."

Hamilton turned down his lips and slowly nodded. "Well, you did good, Rocky. And because of it, I might even let you off for being late... just this once." He winked, and quickly got on with the task at hand, not waiting to see Rocky's response.

Betty, DCI Allen's secretary, explained he was in an important meeting and couldn't be interrupted. Before Hamilton could counter-argue his update was just as important as any meeting taking place, Betty informed him she'd been planning to get in touch with him this morning anyway.

"You've saved me a job, Denis," she said. "DCI Allen wanted me to schedule an appointment with you today."

"Good, because I urgently need to speak to him too, but I don't think I can commit to a time today. I'm just about to drive into Hertfordshire to interview a victim, a possible connection to the bedroom killer case. Could you get him to call me on my mobile whenever he gets out of his meeting please, Betty?"

"Of course, Denis. Leave it with me." She hung up the phone, and Hamilton shouted goodbye to Fraser and Rocky as he left the office.

PC Lakhani was waiting outside the Queen Elizabeth hospital when they arrived, and Hamilton was pleased Rocky had called ahead for them to make the initial introductions.

"The nurses aren't best pleased about all this activity around their patient," Lakhani explained. "But after a brief summary of the case, and how it could possibly connect with the murders in London, they assured us they're more than happy to help."

Hamilton and Clarke followed the PC through the hospital while he briefed them about Brad Royal, his injuries and how he had arrived at the hospital. After interviewing the on-call doctor,

Lakhani discovered Brad had been found unconsciousness three nights ago, and had been in the hospital since that night. The manager of a public house found him bruised and bleeding in the middle of the street and called an ambulance.

"All the details we have are in my report, sir, and I've sent it via email to Rocky already," Lakhani said.

Hamilton was impressed with the rapid progress. They came to a standstill outside a ward, the double doors pushed wide open, secured with rubber stoppers, and the curtains pulled back. Hamilton peered through and counted ten beds, five on each side. The man closest to the window sat in an awkward position – not fully lying down but not sitting upright enough to get a decent view of anything going on around him. Lakhani thumbed towards that same patient.

"That's him, sir, Brad Royal."

Clarke grimaced loudly. "Jesus! Look at the state of him. Is he capable of talking to us?"

Lakhani nodded. "The nurses informed me Brad's been conscious for over twenty-four hours now. I had a brief chat with him earlier and, though some words are difficult to understand over the swelling and facial injuries, he's competent enough."

"Thanks, PC Lakhani, we'll take it from here," Hamilton said, and entered the ward.

Once they announced themselves, Clarke pulled the curtain around the cubicle. Not the ideal private location, but Hamilton knew there was no other choice.

"Mr Royal, we need to speak with you about your wife, Katy."

"What the fuck you wanna talk about her for?" he mumbled through busted lips. "It's me that was flaming well attacked… unless the bitch did this to me! Why would someone give me a good hiding and not even nick my wallet?"

"Can you remember anything before you were attacked, Mr Royal?"

"Yeah… I had a chat with Katy but this fellow got in the way of us. It was late and she ran off, so I thought it was best to leave things to calm down and try again when she was in a better mood. Women, hey! She left me a few months ago, but the truth of the matter is, she'll never get away from me... I'm her husband. Yeah, I can have any woman I want – and have done," he laughed. "There's loads of women like her, but that one will always be mine."

Hamilton groaned. He hated this man already. "The night you were attacked, Mr Royal, what happened once Katy had left?"

"Oh, right, yeah... well I thought, bugger this I need a drink. Walked back to that pub Katy works in to see if it was still open like, but just before I put my hand on the door, I was hit over the head from behind. Never even saw his face. That's the coward's way out, you know? Next thing is I'm waking up here two days later and the police are asking me if I attacked Katy."

"So, you've been told she was attacked?" Clarke asked.

"That Indian copper mentioned something about it, but wouldn't give me any details. I've got a top-notch alibi anyway, haven't I? So, can you tell me... Katy and Frankie, are they okay?"

"They managed to escape the intruder," Hamilton answered.

"Good. That wife of mine sure has grown some balls, so I guess I should be proud. She used to be very submissive and –"

"Mr Royal," Hamilton interrupted, his irritation mounting at yet another arrogant husband to interview on this case; they really gave young men a bad reputation. "Do you know of anyone who would want to harm your wife or son?" He refrained from adding, 'Other than yourself.'

Brad turned down his lips and looked away from the officers, slightly shaking his head. Hamilton wasn't satisfied with the answer and probed the man further, but he continued to evade their glance.

"This is very serious, Mr Royal. We haven't been able to locate your wife and son –"

"She left me, remember? I have no idea what she's been up too *recently*."

The tone of Brad's voice made Hamilton pause. He stared at the patient, the collection of bruises making it difficult to study the facial expression beneath them. But, there was a sense of dishonesty about the man.

"We had hoped you might be able to help us find them," Hamilton finally said.

Brad shrugged, the simple movement evidently an agonising one, judging by the pain etched across his face. Hamilton couldn't help but feel pleased.

"How the hell should I know… at home?" Brad snapped.

"We've checked the apartment and she hasn't been back. However, Katy did mention an old family friend, someone who was like an aunt to her. Do you know who that might be?"

"Oh, that old bag! Should have known Katy would have gone running to her. She used to say the woman was the only connection she still had to her parents, but I made her cut those ties. No point in wallowing in the past."

"The woman's name please, sir," Hamilton said through gritted teeth. It was hard to remain professional when there were degenerates like Brad Royal walking the streets. He clocked his partner's tapping foot and knew Clarke's patience was running just as thin as his own.

"Linda Hill, she lives in Chelsea, down near the Royal Hospital, at least that's where she used to live. Katy said the old woman helped her, interfered is how I'd explain it."

"Thank you for your time," Hamilton said, and pushed his way through the heavy hospital curtains.

He heard Brad shout something uncouth about compensation, but Hamilton chose to ignore it. When they stepped back into the corridor, PC Lakhani was waiting for them.

"We got some useful information from him, but we need to head back to London," Hamilton explained, ready to pass on further instructions and then stopped himself; he wasn't in Charing Cross now.

"No problem, DI Hamilton. I'll deal with as much as I can this end. Just shout if there's anything we can do." Lakhani shook their hands before they left.

"Well, he was a lovely piece of work," Clarke commented once they were away from the ward. Hamilton grumbled, nodding in reply. "Can't really be a coincidence that all three women have men trouble; one's dead and the other two come across as right bastards."

"I doubt it's a coincidence at all, Clarke."

Hamilton reached for his mobile, wanting an exact address for Linda Hill without delay. Before he opened his contact list, Fraser's mobile number appeared on the screen.

"Sir, it's Rocky," the lad said as soon as the call was answered. "I have a name for –"

"Linda Hill, I know. We need an address."

"Already in hand, sir. You're actually on speaker phone now because I'm driving over to the woman's house. Fraser gave me her mobile phone as she thought it would be the easiest form of communication with you."

Hamilton realised there had been no exchange of telephone numbers with Rocky, and thankful Fraser was one step ahead. He asked why she wasn't with him.

"Stayed back at the office, sir, as there were some more files she needed to look at. I thought it would be okay for me to head over to Mrs Hill's address, and at least update Katy Royal on her husband's situation."

"I agree, Rocky, you did the right thing," Hamilton said, in hot pursuit of Clarke as they marched through the hospital and back to the car park. "Stay with Katy and wait for us. We're driving back to London now."

CHAPTER TWENTY

After sitting in mind-numbing A1 traffic, Hamilton was pleased to see Marble Arch in the distance. The iconic London landmark meant they were only a ten-minute drive from the surviving victim, and there was an invisible force urging him to get there faster. The high-pitched ringing of his mobile distracted him.

"DI Hamilton."

"Boss, it's me," Fraser rushed. "Bad news I'm afraid. Rocky's just arrived back at the office."

"Why? Is Katy Royal with him?"

"No, and she wasn't at Linda Hill's home either. Apparently, the woman hasn't seen Katy for months. She gave her some money to help get out of London and hasn't heard from her since. Rocky said the woman was adamant Brad Royal's a bully and Katy had no life with him."

"I could have told you that," he grumbled.

"What, boss?"

"Nothing, never mind." Hamilton mulled over the information as they continued towards Linda's address.

"Anyway, I have some more information, boss," Fraser continued. "The reason I stayed behind earlier is because some of the financial files came back. I haven't had a chance to fully inspect them, but an interesting nugget of information jumped out at me."

Hamilton listened while mouthing to Clarke to pull over, gesturing at an upcoming side-road. They'd have to be watchful of parking attendants; even they weren't above the law when it came to parking on double yellow lines in an unmarked car.

"Before moving to Welwyn, Katy worked as a hairdresser at a salon called Styled Up on Warwick Way… it's a five-minute drive from Scarlett Mitchell's house. And, from the bank records, guess who was a customer once or twice over the last year?"

"Please say Emma Jones."

"Got it in one, boss. So far, it's the best connection we have for all three women."

"I could kiss you!" Hamilton exclaimed, knowing Fraser would take it in the light-hearted way it was meant. "Finally, we have something! Okay, Warwick Way is close to Linda Hill's home, so we'll head straight there instead."

Clarke indicated and pulled back out into the traffic before Hamilton ended the call. He updated his partner as they cruised around London's streets and, surprisingly, found a parking space directly outside the Styled Up salon.

Humidity greeted Hamilton the moment he stepped into the hairdresser's, just as the mixture of dryers and loud music simultaneously attacked his ears. He approached the young woman at reception, unsure of her actual age due to the thickness of her make-up and height of her heels; he never could fathom how women felt comfortable wearing sky-scraping shoes all day. The war paint was another mystery to him.

The pair held out their warrant cards and Hamilton asked to see the manager. The receptionist looked more intrigued than surprised at their request, and as she tottered off on her errand, he rolled his eyes. On numerous occasions, his wife had explained she'd heard the latest snippets of gossip while having her hair blow-dried.

"Hi, I'm Noelle Knight, the manager. Can I help you?"

Hamilton turned to find a tall, slim woman wearing a pair of jeans, ripped at the knees, and a Rolling Stones T-shirt. Her silvery, purple hair was pulled back into a messy bun and she fiddled with a pair of scissors between her fingers; not the image he'd conjured up for a salon manager. He explained why they needed to speak to her, hoping she would invite them into an office or back room.

It was difficult to hear over the various hairdryers being switched on and off at different intervals.

"Follow me," Noelle said, and walked to a workstation where she continued to cut a woman's hair. "Katy worked here for about two years. She was a really lovely person, chatty and fun…. I liked her but… I don't know, I shouldn't really say this, but I think it was obvious she had some problems."

"What do you mean?" Hamilton asked, resigned to the fact they were having the conversation here, or not at all.

"Well, you know, she wouldn't socialise with us much. I mean, she only lived in Bayswater, it's like half an hour from here on the tube. But, she'd never come for a drink and she always rushed home as soon as it hit five o'clock."

"So, would you say she had a strict routine?"

"Hell yeah," Noelle continued. "You could set your watch by Katy. Heaven forbid if an appointment ever ran over. You'd swear if she did something off schedule there'd be hell to pay."

"When did she stop working for you?"

"About six months ago. Not even a bloody warning. Just called me and said she was moving out of London. I gave my other half a right old earache that morning, poor sod. He humoured me and pretended to care, but I could see he had other things on his mind. Anyway, do you know how long it took me to find someone to replace her? Her regulars were not impressed, she was good at her job."

"Speaking of her customers," Hamilton continued. "Did Katy ever see a woman called Emma Jones, or Scarlett Mitchell?"

"Have a chat with Leanne, she'll be able to search our client list on the database for you." She tossed her head back in the direction of the woman at reception.

"Did you ever meet Katy's husband, or see her with anyone else, maybe on her lunch break?"

"Yeah, he picked her up a few times after work and, wow, what a looker. Didn't think shaved head and muscles would be her type. Lunch? I guess she mainly had it in the staff room when she had a few spare minutes. If she did go out, I never noticed her with anyone. Like I said, wasn't a social butterfly. Is everything okay?" She stopped twisting the customer's hair and looked at Hamilton.

"We're trying to locate Katy's whereabouts to help us with an inquiry. If you, or anyone else, hear from her I'd appreciate a call. I'll leave my card at reception."

Noelle smiled and nodded, turning her attention back to the woman in the chair, who'd been fixated on the same page of the magazine the entire time Hamilton was there. As they returned to the reception area, his phone buzzed again. This time it was DCI Allen.

"Clarke, I've got to take this –"

"Go for it, gov. I'll have a chat with Leanne here," he replied, and winked.

Hamilton knew Clarke was a professional, and would never jeopardise their investigation, but just sometimes he worried about his partner's bachelor persona. Still, it wasn't a fact he could dwell on and rushed back outside, relishing the cold air against his face.

"DCI Allen, thanks for getting in touch with me."

"Betty informed me of your message, Denis. But I've just ended my meeting and we've decided we need to hold a press conference about the bedroom killer. I want you present."

"Okay, sir. In that case, you'll need to hear my update now."

Allen remained quiet, grunting in places, while Hamilton divulged information about Katy Royal and her current missing status. The chief was in agreement that she should be included in the press conference, if only as a potential witness at this stage.

"We've just spoken to her previous boss, but we haven't uncovered anything much of value," Hamilton said. "To be honest, I'm thinking if she didn't return to Linda Hill's house, which was the intention, I can't see any reason why she'd come back here. We're waiting to see if there are any hits on the computers for the other two female victims."

"Okay, Denis. Get onto the team at Welwyn and ask them to check the hospital's CCTV. If we can get a still image of Katy Royal leaving the area, then we can circulate it to the press."

"Yes, sir. When is the conference scheduled for?"

"In two hours, at Scotland Yard. We want to ensure it makes the evening news. I'll see you there."

Before Hamilton could protest about the short time frame, the phone line went dead. He rushed back into the hairdresser's, the same mugginess engulfing him, and collided with his partner.

"I'm afraid Leanne doesn't have much for us," Clarke said. "She could confirm Emma Jones' previous appointments, none of which were ever with Katy, and she also hasn't been here for months. Scarlett Mitchell isn't on the database at all."

His partner stepped around him and opened the door. Hamilton held up his hand and thanked the receptionist. He stopped suddenly, his eyes drawn to a noticeboard he hadn't observed earlier. Frowning, his mind raced as he reached over and selected one of the many business cards pinned to the board.

"Do you mind if I keep this?" he asked the wannabe cover girl.

"Go for it. We've got loads," Leanne replied, and returned to flicking the pages of her glossy magazine.

Once they were outside, Clarke questioned what the chief's call had been about. Before answering and relaying all the details, Hamilton slid the business card into his coat pocket. There was something he needed to review when they returned to the incident room.

CHAPTER TWENTY-ONE

Fraser parked the car outside Katy Royal's address and cut the engine. It was a peaceful, residential street made up of mostly terraced houses, with the exception of the apartments at the end of the road, which backed onto a huge country park. An ideal place to raise a family, Fraser thought, but quickly shook the fantasy away. She'd been so busy fulfilling her career goals, being single had become a way of life for her.

Rocky and PC Lakhani followed her to the apartment block, and while the men browsed the various names and numbers on the intercom panel, Fraser pushed open the heavy black door.

"Smarty pants," Rocky said with a smile, and they entered the building.

An hour earlier, when Hamilton had visited Linda Hill after leaving Styled Up, he had requested the woman file a missing person's report. While, at the same time in Welwyn, Lakhani took a similar statement from Brad Royal. With the possible threat to Katy and Frankie, their disappearance was graded as a high alert. Meanwhile, Fraser and Rocky travelled to Welwyn to find sufficient information in preparation of the evening's press conference.

"You have the keys, right?" Fraser confirmed.

"Yes, Katy gave them to me the night she was attacked," PC Lakhani replied. "One more flight of stairs and it's the door on the left."

The trio stopped outside apartment six and Fraser took the keys. Before opening the door, she banged heavily and called Katy's name, informing the woman of their identity. When no reply came, she unlocked the door.

Fraser inspected the bathroom, noting the bottles of blonde hair dye and, using clear evidence bags, collected the two toothbrushes on the sink. She also looked in the bin, but it was empty. Making her way back into the hall, she glimpsed the stained blood on the wall that they were still awaiting results from.

PC Lakhani joined her from the living room, holding a photograph. "In the absence of anything of quality from the hospital CCTV, this could be used for the press conference. It's a perfect shot of Katy and her son."

"DI Hamilton won't be pleased. He really thought we'd get a lead from the hospital image."

"The exterior camera faced outward away from the hospital, and so had only caught the back of Katy Royal's head. Worse still, it didn't catch the car she jumped into. It was a foolish error on my part, not to get the number plate, but I only realised it was her inside after it was too late. It was a dark Toyota, but I know that doesn't help."

Fraser looked at her watch and groaned. "Honestly, I really don't think we're going to make it back to London before DCI Allen is interviewed; the rush-hour traffic on the A1 will be manic. But maybe... do you think you could get back to your station and email a copy over to my boss within the next half hour or so?"

"Of course, it's only a twenty-minute walk from here. Rocky's got the victim's laptop and mobile phone. I'll go and log all this for evidence as well."

Fraser thanked him, and he left to go and discuss the plan of action with Rocky. Just as her foot stepped into the smaller of the two bedrooms, Fraser heard a woman's voice outside in the corridor, and she rushed out to see who was there.

"Can I help you, ma'am?" she called out to the figure climbing the stairs.

The woman stopped and looked over her shoulder. "Erm... no... just on my way home."

"Barefoot?" Fraser replied, forcing the woman to turn around and face her. "What's your name?"

"Alexina Golding... I live upstairs. I just heard the noises down here and was being a bit nosey is all. Sorry. I must get back indoors, my kids will cause a riot without me there."

Fraser stood on the first step, bringing herself closer to the woman. "If I could just ask you about your neighbour –"

"I don't like leaving the kids..."

"I can come upstairs with you, it's no problem," she said, and took a further step up.

The woman hesitated and glanced upstairs before meeting Fraser's stare. "Okay, but quickly while they're quiet."

"We haven't been able to locate Katy Royal, your neighbour from number six. Do you know where she is?"

Alexina shrugged. "I've been away for a few days, so I really wouldn't know."

"Do you know if Katy had any friends in the area that she might be staying with?"

"No, she was really quiet. I don't know much about her if I'm honest. Sorry I can't help you more."

Fraser handed the woman a business card and asked her to call if anyone returned to the apartment. Alexina snatched it and ran the last few stairs up to the next landing, but then stopped abruptly and turned.

"Is everything okay? With Katy and her son, I mean..." the woman mumbled.

Fraser smiled, in an attempt to reassure the neighbour. But, then when she thought of Katy and Frankie's faces being shown on the evening news, it didn't feel right to lie.

"We hope so. They're currently missing and it's imperative we find Mrs Royal. Please do call me if you think of anything."

Rocky and PC Lakhani's deep voices drew nearer and it broke the connection between Fraser and Alexina. When she looked back up the stairwell, the woman had gone. She rejoined the men and Rocky confirmed the lack of evidence in the apartment. They were still awaiting forensic reports from the night of the alleged attack, but he'd secured the main items Hamilton had been interested in.

"Had another thought," he continued. "Katy Royal worked in The Tavern pub. It's where her husband was left for dead and the manager found him. So, I was thinking…"

"Worth us paying him a visit, while we're here," Fraser finished Rocky's sentence.

"Great minds."

Happy to make his own way back to the station, PC Lakhani gave Fraser directions to the pub and noted down Hamilton's email address. She was beginning to enjoy working with these Hertfordshire officers; they couldn't do enough to help with the investigation.

Inside The Tavern, Fraser was surprised by its emptiness. She had never walked into a pub in London and been greeted by only one member of bar staff and one patron. Rocky had mentioned the pub aimed itself more at serving the locals and so, the pair found themselves stood at the bar for a few minutes ignored by the tall, slim barman. He had his back to them, tapping aggressively on the screen of his iPhone.

"Service!" Rocky roared.

The man spun around, his face flushed red and he wiped the sweat from his brow. He dithered, mumbling and eyeing his phone.

"PC O'Connor and DS Fraser. We'd like to speak to the manager."

"Yes, that's me. Craig Gillan. What's this about?"

"We believe Katy Royal works for you?"

"Oh, her, yeah. She ain't here."

The man lowered his phone and casually leaned his elbow on an ale tap lever. Rocky and Fraser exchanged glances. She raised her eyebrows, hoping her new partner would understand; he did, and continued the conversation with the bar manager.

"Do you know where she is?"

"Not a bloody clue."

"And you're not worried that she hasn't shown up for work?"

Craig grunted. "She wouldn't be the first barmaid to fly off with no warning. This is hardly the Ibiza club scene," he said, outstretching his arm across the quiet room.

"So, it doesn't seem out of character? Was she due into work?" Rocky questioned.

"Well... she had a few days off. But I've been trying to call her, as I need her in for this evening's shift... I've got things to do," Craig replied and glanced down at his phone.

"When's the last time you saw Katy?"

"I think it was Thursday, just before she finished her shift. She called the next day asking for the weekend off. She's worked hard, so I agreed."

"Is there anyone she was particularly friendly with in the bar? Or maybe someone she didn't get along with?"

Craig turned down his lips and shrugged, pressing the button on his phone and watching the screen come to life. After a couple of seconds, he looked up.

"Waiting for a call?" Fraser interrupted.

"Can't get hold of my son is all."

"And your son is?"

"Neil. Neil Smith... he took his mother's surname. I need some help behind the bar, as I've said, I've got a prior engagement I can't get out of. Thought I'd see if the boy wanted some extra cash," he said and rubbed his hand over the greying stubble on his cheek.

The only other person in the bar finally made himself known by rattling his empty glass on the wooden bar top. Craig took his prompt and began pouring the man a fresh pint.

"I hear you're asking about Katy's friends," the patron called out.

"And you are?" Rocky stepped forward, bridging the gap between them.

"Ah, I'm John Lynch... no one of any interest, lad. But, I'm always propping up this bar, the perks of retirement you see. Anyway, I'm not sure I'd call him a friend, but there was a new guy in here Thursday night and he's the first person I've noticed our Katy take any interest in. In the past, if anyone new came in, and trust me that doesn't happen often, one of us would send him packing... Katy isn't the type of barmaid to flirt."

"But she was Thursday night?" Rocky asked.

"Do you know who the man is?" Fraser added.

John laughed and took a few gulps from his pint of Guinness before answering. Fraser noticed Craig's phone was gripped firmly in his hand again.

"Right, to answer your questions... Firstly, I've never seen the woman talk to one man the entire night, so I'm going to hedge my bets and say yes, she was interested. And secondly, no, I'm not sure who he is. I definitely heard the name Matthew, but I can't remember if I've seen him in here before... Hmmm, just not sure. Sorry."

"Could you describe what he looked like?" Rocky asked, and grabbed a notebook and pen from his jacket pocket.

"A bit like you, lad. Tall, white, dark hair. His face was clean shaven though," John replied, nodding his head toward Rocky. "Oh, I did notice a tattoo... the word mum, and a date, on his wrist. Left wrist. Yeah. I'm pretty sure." He took another swig of his pint.

Fraser turned to Craig. "Do you know anyone called Matthew who drinks in here?"

"Sorry, love, I don't."

"Do you have CCTV? In or outside of the pub?"

Craig shook his head slowly. "'Fraid not. It's an unneeded expense for a small local like this. We all know each other."

"Except Matthew," Fraser countered.

"Well, yes," Craig shrugged. "Must be new in town if I haven't met him yet. Anyway, is there anything else I can help you with? I am kinda busy."

She raised her eyebrows and slowly glanced at all the empty chairs. The manager huffed.

"You found a man beaten pretty badly outside your pub last week –"

"And I've given a full statement to the police! I didn't hear or see anything. I found him when I was locking up. You should have all this information."

"Were you alone?"

Craig shuffled, the phone screen flashing in his hand. "Yes, I was. Look, there's really nothing more I can add to what I've already told the officers. So, if you don't mind?"

"Of course, thank you for your time," Fraser said and reached into her pocket.

She slid two business cards across the bar and asked the men to call her, or the Welwyn police station if they came into contact with Katy. The pair needed to get back to London without any further delay. Hamilton would want to know about the mysterious man, Matthew, and The Tavern's fidgety manager before the press conference.

CHAPTER TWENTY-TWO

The smell of blood grabbed Katy's attention first. Then the thick tape masking her painful groans, and the restrictive rope bound tightly around her wrists and ankles. The braided material scorched her skin with the slightest movement. She repeatedly fluttered her eyelids, forcing them to open, regardless of their protest. A shooting pain from her neck travelled up into her head, making it difficult to focus.

Katy lay on the carpeted floor in a foetal position, her right side taking all her weight. Her arms, awkwardly tied behind her back, made it impossible to move. She squinted and gazed around. Instantly knowing where she was, Katy tried to scream. Her muffled noise did nothing but elevate the pain radiating throughout her entire body.

Her mind scrambled back to images of the street, of being grabbed from behind and then Brad's bloodstained face came crashing to the forefront of her mind. Katy's chest tightened, adding further pressure to the already difficult task of breathing. She barked her son's name through the tape again, and again, until her throat itched and she coughed into the shield covering her mouth. Laughter echoed from behind.

Katy's heart raced as fast as her brain and she cursed herself. *Why can't I remember what happened?*

Clouding her thoughts were Brad's menacing eyes staring back at her. She blinked his face away, trying to concentrate on the dark room, dimly lit by a lone lamp in the corner. The murmur of the television in the background, the familiar opening credits of the evening news. The snigger came again.

She wiggled, but her body was almost unresponsive to her instruction. A numbing sensation trickled down her arm and leg.

While listening to every single noise, her eyes finally widened and she examined every shape she could within the dark room. The dark living room. Her heart sank. Katy pulled in as much air as she could through her nose and yanked her body, using her feet to scrape around the floor a few inches. The effort left Katy exhausted, her own panting thundered in her ears. Her right arm pained under the slow movement of her full weight and she stopped, dropping her head uncomfortably to the floor and cried.

Tears fell from her lashes, wetting the crusted blood which had gushed from her nose hours earlier. Fear bubbled in her stomach, spreading out to every part of her body until the nausea took over. She gagged, sucking the tape into her mouth, no choice but to swallow back the vomit.

"Where is my son? Where is Frankie?" she babbled into the masking tape.

A low groan came from just beyond her head. Mocking her, she thought, and she clamped her eyes shut. Katy only needed to pull herself around a few more shuffles, and she'd be face to face with the owner of the laugh. She exhaled, drained and petrified of who stood behind her, unable to conquer her confusion, and lacking the strength to confront it.

"Mum," a small voice called in the distance.

Katy's head snapped up and she grumbled a reply. It was Frankie. An overwhelming urge to find her son jump-started her body into action. She kicked her feet, wrestling with the floor as quickly as she could. A loud sound of jeans chafing together as footsteps pounded past her. Doors banged. Ignoring the pain, Katy finally spun full circle. She froze, craving to hear Frankie's voices again. A door further down the hallway slammed again. Silence.

Unexpectedly, the overhead light switched to life and Katy recoiled; the brightness violated her sensitive eyes. She angled her body, pulling her head up as high as possible and opened her eyes. A deep wail escaped through the masking tape and she collapsed back to the floor. There, in the armchair ahead of her, with dried bloodstains to his temple and hairline, sat Matthew.

CHAPTER TWENTY-THREE

Five years ago

Matthew knelt beside his mother and gently squeezed her frail hand. He knew that approaching his mid-thirties and still having the love of a mother, was a joy not to be taken for granted. So many of his friends hadn't had the same privilege, but right there in that moment, it did nothing to comfort him. The thought of the impending goodbye caused his heart rate to race; his chest already felt too heavy to move. He lowered his head to their entwined fingers, his mind a blank canvas, unable to concentrate on a single memory.

He could barely breathe, and pulled up his head to inhale a lungful of air. He wanted to run as fast as possible, let his legs guide him to any other place but this room he was rooted to. But, his body was like deadwood, and he was helpless against the suffocation of his mother's dying sighs.

He gazed over at the glass dresser, adorned with her favourite perfumes and creams. The flowery, towelling dressing gown, hanging from its home on the back of the door, and the flowery wallpaper, tinged yellow from decades of smoking. His mother had never touched a cigarette in her life, but they were both passive smokers to his father's disgusting habit. Matthew looked down and rubbed his thumb over the faded scar on his mother's hand. One of the many wounds she'd suffered in a bid to save Matthew. The only visible one he could remember since he'd been a teenager.

She had saved his life on more occasions than he cared to think about, or wanted to think about for that matter. Silently tormented at the hand of her husband, until the day Matthew realised he had grown larger and stronger and could overpower the old man. It had been a Saturday night and the theme tune to Blind Date echoed through their living room as he pinned his father to the wall. Both of Matthew's hands had wrapped forcefully around the man's neck. That night, his mother's screams had dragged him back to his senses and he'd released his father. She had saved both the men in her life. Matthew's father hadn't touched a drop of alcohol since, that Matthew knew of, but he'd never forgiven the man for how he'd treated his mother.

Matthew exhaled slowly. Sorrow, rather than the suppressed anger, weighed heavily on him now. He could hear his father whistling the tune of some television programme downstairs, while his mother waited for death to greet her, and he wondered if his father could ever return to the violent monster he once was. Matthew's hands shook when he thought of his own life choices.

"What's the matter, my son? You're trembling."

He flinched, his mother's gentle voice catching him off guard. With his finger, he seized the lone tear before it fell from his eye. It felt unfair to make his mother watch him cry.

"I'm fine, Mum."

The smile didn't reach her eyes, her grey skin almost featureless. She groaned as she turned her head to face his. His eyes glazed over with involuntary tears and he clenched his teeth, pushing the emotions back down.

"What have I told you… mothers know everything… there's no point even trying to lie…"

Her voice trailed off and she closed her eyes. Matthew held his breath, waiting to hear if her next one would come.

"I remember when you were just five years old," she whispered, her eyes remaining shut. "The two of us had a day out… just me and you, no one else. I took you to London Zoo… you loved all the animals. We had ice cream, big mounds of the stuff until our bellies turned into creamy volcanoes." She paused, unable to hear Matthew's sobs over her giggles. "You didn't want to come home. Your father had just lost his job and… that's when the drinking started. You knew what it meant, even at that young age, and you didn't… you just didn't want to come home, said you'd rather we lived in the zoo. The animals were kinder than people, you said… You wanted it to be just mummy and Matthew…"

He opened his mouth and let the moans escape; he couldn't hide the sadness from her any longer. Using the back of his hand, Matthew wiped the wet stains from his cheeks and told his mother he would take her to London Zoo again. He wanted to thank her for saving him from some of the darkest moments in his life. He needed her to know he was a good person, and how monumentally she had saved him from making some of the most awful decisions throughout his life. But it was too late.

Matthew gazed down at his mother's withering face, He didn't need to listen for her next breath. He watched the last, shallow gasp slip from her lips. Her chest stopped rising and falling, and her fingers slowly fell away from his. It was soothing to know his mother was no longer in pain, but his heart broke regardless.

The walls closed in around him, the air evaporated. Matthew stood up and ran from his mother's bedroom, from the house he'd called home his entire life. It was no longer safe there with his father, without her. A part of Matthew died with his mother, and he knew he'd never be the same again.

CHAPTER TWENTY-FOUR

Hamilton stood at the back of the crowded room and observed the scene before him. The artificial lighting cast a stark glow onto the faces of those sitting at the long, narrow table. The various camera shutters sounded like gunfire as photographers fought for the best shot, even though their subjects were barely moving. The mix of voices contended with one another for attention, and when information was given, it only led to question after relentless question.

In the two hours since their last conversation, Hamilton had gathered the required details and travelled to Scotland Yard, just in time to update DCI Allen. Audrey had visited the incident room while half his team were in Welwyn. Sitting in his office, she confirmed that both women suffered sexual assaults before they were murdered, and the DNA from the pubic hair and the sample found on the wool were a match. It proved the husbands they had interviewed were no longer suspects, but Hamilton's frustration mounted when Audrey continued to explain the owner of the DNA was not on the system. The statements from Brad Royal and Linda Hill had escalated the missing person's warning to high alert, and now Hamilton's concern intensified. He also distributed the image of mother and son to the relevant contacts before the press conference began.

With details leaked prior to the meeting, Hamilton wasn't at all surprised to find the questions being fired at the chief related to the bedroom killer. Unsure where the holes in his department or station were, he wondered if those involved felt guilty when journalists sometimes misinterpreted an investigation. His mind briefly drifted to his daughter, and how Maggie's beautiful face had made front page news. If a detective inspector couldn't save his own daughter, was the community really safe at all? Hamilton blew out a large puff of air and rubbed his eyes, forcing himself to return his attention to the conference.

"We are confident Scarlett and Noah Mitchell, and Emma and Kyle Jones were murdered by the same person within the last two months," DCI Allen's voice boomed into the microphone. A moment of stillness took hold of the room. "Both women were in their thirties and single parents living in the Islington and Pimlico areas of London. We are appealing to anyone who knew these women, or may have seen and spoken to them since June. DNA evidence has been recovered from both crime scenes, therefore we're confident we can eliminate suspects."

A murmur spread through the crowd, the journalists impatient as their urge to ask questions increased. DCI Allen raised his hand, regaining control of the room.

"You have all been given a photograph of Katy and Frankie Royal," the chief continued. "The woman in the photo now has short, blonde hair and was seen last night leaving Queen Elizabeth hospital in Welwyn, in a dark Toyota car. If anyone has any information regarding this, we would like them to get in touch. It is crucial we find them."

"Why?" a voice yelled from the front row. "How are they connected to the murders?"

"Katy is a single mother who was attacked in her home. We believe it could be the same man and –"

"What's the connection between London and Welwyn?" the journalist interrupted the chief, and Hamilton spied a flash of anger in his superior's eyes.

"At this stage, we haven't confirmed a connection." Allen raised his hand again, refusing another interruption. "However, I can tell you, as of six months ago, Katy lived and worked in London, and we are investigating all possible avenues. It is of the utmost urgency we find these two missing people. We have supplied you with images of all the victims, and we would appreciate your assistance in catching this criminal, before he attacks another vulnerable mother and child in their home. Thank you for your time."

Hamilton overheard further opinions and expressions shared as the press conference came to a close. Journalists were never pleased when they weren't given a chance to grill the man in charge. He wondered if any of them had considered jobs in the Metropolitan Police, as so many of their valid questions were often left unanswered. He slipped out of the small room, pulling at his shirt collar as he escaped to the front entrance. Once outside, the night sky greeted him and he inhaled the cold air. It wasn't long before Allen escaped too.

"Walking back to the station, Denis?" the chief asked.

"Yes, sir, most of us will be working into the night with this case. I think the team are going to order a pizza or two."

As the pair walked along the Strand, with Trafalgar Square on the horizon, Hamilton was suddenly very grateful for the short distance and brisk walk.

"How are things, Denis? The Everett case… and the possible effect it could have on you, it was an oversight on my behalf. I apologise."

"That's all been dealt with, sir… there's no need to bring it up again. I'm fully aware that working in the division I do, that death is a part of my everyday life. If I crumbled at the sight of every dead body that reminded me of Maggie… Well, I wouldn't be a very useful detective inspector, now would I?"

"No, you're quite right. How is Elizabeth?"

"Good, thanks. She's looking forward to seeing you and Mrs Allen at this year's Christmas dinner."

"Oh, don't mention the C-word, Denis. It's far too early in the year to even think of that. I also wanted to let you know I've had an update about Dixon, the sergeant you're waiting for. Well, I'm pleased to say she'll be joining the team next week. She's MIT, but transferring from Kingston."

Hamilton nodded as they turned onto Agar Street and climbed the steps to Charing Cross Police Station entrance. He let his hand linger on the door handle.

"Have you spoken to Les Wedlock, sir?"

Allen sighed. "Yes. It's not looking good with his mother's condition, I'm afraid. The stroke has meant she needs around the clock care. He's staying in Kent for the time being, might even request a transfer to the local station there."

"I spoke to him last night as well, but I hadn't realised it could be a permanent move for him."

"Well, not to worry, we'll look into how it affects your team and what can be done to minimise any further disruption. You must understand though, I can't make any promises on that front, Denis."

The chief tipped his head towards the door, signalling the end of their conversation. Hamilton opened it and let Allen pass. Standing back, he watched the chief walk away and join another colleague. In this profession, change was inevitable; colleagues moved from one division to the next, and from one investigation to another on a regular basis. Although he was never one to get emotionally attached to people, he had to admit to a touch of melancholy at the thought of losing two respected team members in as many weeks.

Hamilton shoved his hands into his coat pockets as he took the stairs up to the incident room. His fingers wrapped around the thin piece of card he'd placed there earlier and his eyes widened in disbelief. Springing into action, he bolted up the remaining steps two at a time, overtly cursing his forgetfulness and barging past a young uniformed officer. With the business card squeezed inside his fist, Hamilton worried his absentmindedness may have delayed a vital piece of information being uncovered.

Fraser and Rocky had returned from Welwyn. She was busy updating the evidence board when Hamilton interrupted her as she wrote a question mark next to the name Matthew.

"I need you to look into this company, and find out if our victims are connected to it in any way, Fraser," he said, handing her the business card. "I picked it up at the hairdresser's and I remember seeing one clipped to the fridge in Scarlett Mitchell's apartment too. It could be a coincidence, but there seems to be a few too many of those in this case and I don't want to overlook it."

"Of course, boss," she replied. "And, speaking of coincidences, I don't think you're going to like this…"

"Go on."

"Rocky and I had a brief look through the internet history on Katy Royal's computer, she too visited a few chat rooms and online friendship sites. But, unless the man is using different information, profile picture and name… I can't find anyone linking the women together."

"That can't be a coincidence," Rocky said. "Two murders and one attempted murder victim all chatting to men online, and you're saying not one of them is our guy?"

"Well, no…. but I can't find one person all three have been in contact with."

Hamilton frowned. "Listen, online dating or friendship, or whatever it's called, is not my cup of tea. However, I'm sure the majority of the population have, at some point in the decade or so, had a conversation with someone online. The number of people I've heard of who meet up and are now married… So, yes, while they can undoubtedly pose a threat, it's just not uncommon for people to be engaging in these types of relationships."

"I'm not," Fraser and Rocky chimed together.

Clarke laughed, and pointed between his colleagues. "Getting divorced, and single for how many years now?"

Fraser rolled her eyes and smirked. Hamilton guessed she'd rather give Clarke the finger, but she remained professional, as always. She broke away from the group, busy examining the business card and tapping away at the computer. Hamilton joined Rocky who had two laptops opened on the desk.

"Is this Katy Royal's?" he asked.

"Yes, sir. I'm just having another look through her search history. From her recent purchases, it looks like she was preparing to protect herself from someone."

"Are there any personal photos on there?"

Rocky's hands moved quickly over the cursor, clicking buttons and searching folders, but found nothing. The officer switched his attention to the mobile phone in a clear bag.

"Luckily, the phone doesn't have a passcode on it, sir," Rocky said. "There's no photos on the laptop, but here, there's quite a few on this."

Hamilton accepted Katy's mobile phone and thumbed through a variety of photographs of the Royal family. His eyes roamed over the thumbnails, flicking back and forth over a couple before he hesitated.

"Damn it," he yelled, and peered at his watch. "The hairdresser's will be closed now."

"Sorry, sir?"

"The manager… this is not how she described Brad Royal. I didn't pick up on it because, well, everyone changes their appearance over the years." Hamilton punched the table. "Rocky, see if you can get an address for Noelle Knight, the owner of Styled Up. Then, I want you to get yourself round there and show her these photographs, confirm if he's the man she regularly saw Katy Royal with. If it's not, I want a full description of him and the car he drove."

"Didn't she say Brad was bald?" Clarke asked

"Exactly. Except I can't find one picture of Katy's husband on this phone without a full head of blonde hair. And there's hundreds of images stored here."

"So, perhaps that night in The Tavern wasn't the first time Katy met this Matthew guy?"

Hamilton folded his arms, cupping his chin between his thumb and forefinger and examined the evidence board. He wondered, as vile as Brad Royal had appeared, if perhaps Katy had fled the city because she'd been involved with another man.

CHAPTER TWENTY-FIVE

Hamilton sat in his office, drumming his fingers on the mahogany desk. Relying on members of the public wasn't always easy and Lindsay, the woman who'd answered his last telephone call, was the epitome of unhelpfulness. In twenty minutes or so, she told him, a senior member of staff would return his call. It had only been four minutes since he'd hung up, but the frustration spread from his temples and shattered the back of his head.

To calm his hands, Hamilton picked up his mobile phone and sent an apologetic text message to his wife. Apart from that one emotional morning, they had barely spoken during the past week. Rushing past each other as Elizabeth left for the school where she was headmistress, or tiptoeing into bed because she was already asleep. She never moaned when he explained he wouldn't be home for dinner, or that he couldn't be entirely certain what time he'd return. Elizabeth had grown accustomed to leaving a plate of food for her husband in the fridge.

With calls coming in from the earlier press conference and Hamilton waiting for information, he knew it could be an all-nighter at the station. Within minutes his wife had replied: *No problem, Den! I love you xx*

"Boss!" Fraser interrupted. "I've found something."

Hamilton smiled briefly, ditched his phone and followed the sergeant into the incident room. There were reams of paperwork scattered over her desk, and Rocky still hadn't returned.

"I went back through the financial information we had," Fraser said, her hands lingering over highlighted sheets. "Emma Jones had an account with the company and frequently paid them via PayPal. Now, there's no paper trail from Scarlett Mitchell, so I'm assuming she used cash."

"And Katy Royal?"

"Nearly every day during the week while she was living in London, but no activity with them since she moved."

"Right, I'm waiting for the manager to call me ba–" His phone shrilled in the distance and he took flight, only realising it was his mobile ringing once inside the office.

"Rocky, what have you got?"

"I'm on my way back to the station now, sir, but I thought you'd want to know ASAP. Noelle Knight confirmed Brad Royal is not the man she saw with Katy. Appearance wise, she couldn't tell me anything new, but said he may have had a tattoo on his arm; again, vague with details."

"Good. Okay, see you shortly."

Ending one call, Hamilton switched his focus to the office phone which had started ringing. He yanked the receiver and introduced himself.

"Hello, I'm Sebastian Harvey. I'm the owner of Embassy Taxis."

"Thank you for calling me back, Mr Harvey." Hamilton perched on the desk.

"Am I in trouble?"

"I hope not. I'm looking for information. We're confident two of our victims were customers of your company."

"I'm sure I can get you any information you require. Our records are all online, with most customers now choosing cashless payments through our app, it's a useful way of storing all their personal information."

"Would you still have the details of the journeys they took, and the driver?"

"It would depend on the time frame you're looking at. For a variety of reasons, we're obligated to clear our history and some information. Years worth of London routes would be too much to keep."

"The last twelve months."

"Possibly, yes. My company is three years old, but the trend of paying for your taxi via PayPal or Apple Pay has only escalated in the last year or so. I would have to look into it for you, if you can give me their names?"

"No, I won't give you sensitive information over the phone, Mr Harvey. What I will do is send a colleague of mine over to you immediately."

Mr Harvey informed Hamilton he was working from home, but had all the equipment and information needed there to hand. He wrote a note with the man's address on and stood up, signalling for Clarke from the office doorway.

"Before I go, do you have a driver named Matthew?"

Mr Harvey paused on the line for a few moments, as Clarke took the piece of paper from his boss. Hamilton nodded towards Rocky as he entered the incident room, and mouthed to his partner to take the young officer with him.

"I have no employee called Matthew," the man finally answered.

"Matt?"

"No."

"Okay, thank you for returning my call. I'm sending two detectives out to you, they'll be with you shortly."

"There's just one thing playing on my mind… and it's such a coincidence that you called me really."

Hamilton rolled his eyes at yet another unfavourable C-word rearing its ugly head, but nevertheless, encouraged the man to continue.

"Well, I watched this evening's news, and it could be nothing, but…" Mr Harvey paused. "I do have one driver who works for me. He's worked full-time, mainly on the day shift, for over three years. Then about three months ago, he reduced his shifts, wanting to work on some sort of freelance capacity. Strange really, as he'd been all about routine in his life previous to that."

"Why do you think that's connected to our case?"

"Because he said he'd found a job in Welwyn… and he drives a navy Toyota Arius. I mean, I was going to call –"

"I need his name!" Hamilton demanded.

His heartbeat drummed faster the more Mr Harvey spoke. After he'd ordered the man to give his colleagues all the necessary details for that particular driver, Hamilton ended the call and marched back into the incident room. He requested the help of the remaining officers in the room and updated them, along with Fraser, about the conversation he'd just had with Mr Harvey.

"I want everything we can find on this Pete Campbell. Find out if he's on our systems, where he lives, and what this other job is in Welwyn. And I want an image of him too, the salon manager may recognise him."

The detectives scribbled notes while Hamilton made his instructions clear. He wasn't in the habit of pulling on extra resources without initial approval, but this investigation needed it. Hoping DCI Allen was still in the building, he left the busy team while he went in search of the chief to update him.

CHAPTER TWENTY-SIX

The flick of the light switch had been a tease. No sooner had Katy identified Matthew's figure, the room was cloaked in darkness once again. His scent wafted up her nostrils as he crept closer. Leather boots crunched under his every step. He slipped his large hands under her arms and pulled her up and, in one swift movement, yanked her feet off the ground and carried her from the room. With her arms still tied behind her back, he pinned her in place against his body. Katy wept.

"Shh, now. Don't fight this any longer," he whispered, his hot breath burning tracks down her cheek as he nuzzled into her hair.

She rested her head on his broad chest, her body still and calm, but inside she was screaming. Katy's attention dashed in every direction, demanding escape plans and fight tactics and secret stealth manoeuvres she'd seen so many actresses conquer in films. Nothing came but a blanket of empty thoughts. She felt her body give up as he lowered her down onto the bed. She squeezed her eyes shut, images of Matthew's limp body fastened with rope to the armchair in the next room came to her now.

"Look at me," he said.

Katy obeyed his demand. His eyes bore down onto her as he stood at the foot of the bed. She couldn't pull herself from his gaze to look around, but she knew exactly where she was. The room was exactly how she'd left it six months before. The sound of her own heavy breathing filled her ears until they ached. The pain in her arms she ignored.

"Why are you doing this to me?"

He sighed, and sat next to her on the bed. She lifted her head to follow him, but the strain was too much and it flopped back.

"After all this time… how can you still not understand?" he said.

Katy stared at the ceiling, her arms numb and legs too weak to kick out. She gazed to either side of her, but there was nothing to help.

"I… I don't know…"

He spun around, kneeling on the floor beside her and grabbed her face. "Look at me."

"I am." Tears strolled down her face. "Pete… I see you. But… why?"

"You don't see me," he spat. "All these years!" He pushed her face away, stood up and paced the floor. "I've looked after you, watched over you. And just when I thought you were ready to let me back into your life, you ran away from me again."

Katy's T-shirt quivered as her chest rose and fell. She strained her neck, allowing her eyes to follow Pete around the room. She couldn't understand him.

"But, years? Pete… it's only been weeks since –"

He roared laughing and pulled his long, dark hair. Walking over to the dressing table, he muttered something to himself over and over again, but Katy couldn't turn her head far enough to see what he was doing. A mechanical humming noise filled the air.

"Of course! Stupid. Stupid. Stupid," he repeated.

Laughing again, Pete returned to her line of vision. Brandishing hair clippers and a vanity mirror, he roughly attacked his head. Clumps of hair whizzed through the air, falling onto her body, the bed and floor. Katy couldn't contain her fear any longer and she wailed, not wanting to watch as he turned the tool onto his face, stripping away his black beard. When he was eventually finished, Pete flung his arms apart and beamed at her. Though his appearance was far from immaculate, Katy gasped as she recognised the man behind the disguise.

"Now you see me."

She bit her lip, attempting to control the erratic sobs and nodded her head repeatedly. They were interrupted by Frankie's screams, calling her name from the next bedroom. Her eyes widened.

"Let me see my son!" Katy yelled.

Pete sauntered over to the door and firmly closed it. "We're not finished yet."

He placed the tools down and lay next to Katy on the bed. Stroking her cheek lightly with one finger, he began singing Adele's *Someone Like You*.

"Why are you doing this?" she repeated.

"I was stupid to have let you go all those years ago. If only I hadn't let you leave me that morning, you would have been mine. We would have been together. Then… a miracle happened, and you walked back into my life."

Katy frowned, her confusion escalated with his every word. She wanted to kick out, scream, or even understand Pete's cryptic memories, but the murmur of Frankie's distant cries kept her from questioning the man.

"Never mind, I'll find someone like you," she sang.

Tears shimmered in his eyes. "You do remember… I knew I shouldn't have played games in London, you must forgive me. The first time you got in my taxi, I should have told you it was me. I was… scared. What if you didn't remember? What if you rejected me again? I was happy watching you… you intrigue and surprise me every day. But then…" Pete's upper lip snarled like a dog's. "Then I saw your husband and how he frightened you that night, and I had to get rid of him."

Katy glared at him. "You? You put Brad in hospital?"

"Yes! I was late getting to you that night from London… I'm so sorry. After you ran off I followed Brad and took care of him for you. But, then you did it to me again." His anger was replaced with pain. "You started seeing that loser in the room next door, you even said you'd love to see him again, in front of me… in front of me! Why, Katy? Were you trying to make me jealous?"

"Untie me," Katy whispered.

Pete sniffed, wiped away the unshed tears and sat up. She could see he was battling with her request and she didn't want to aggravate him. He drummed his fingers on his chin, scanning her body up and down.

"I just... I mean... how can I show you I remember, if you keep me tied up like this?"

While she continued to hum Adele's tune, Pete reached down and yanked the rope from her ankles. As Katy's legs begrudgingly extended, a burning sensation ran down them. He straddled her thighs, released her wrists and sat back to allow her upper body to straighten up. She opened out her arms, desperate to be relieved from the weight of him. He leaned forward and lightly kissed her bare neck. Her jaw tightened as she draped her arms over his back. Her stomach clenched, restraining the tears.

"I was so frightened," he groaned. "So frightened I'd never find you again. I knew if I followed that dimwit of a husband of yours that he'd eventually lead me back to you."

Pete slightly lifted himself away from her, his mouth curved into a smile. He rested on one elbow while his other hand trailed down her body, his fingers skimming over her breasts and navel until they reached the cusp of her trousers. Katy screeched. Diving forward she shoved both thumbs into each of his eyes. Pete fell onto his side howling. She thrashed her legs out from under him and, wriggling free, jabbed her knee into his genitals before stumbling towards the door.

Katy sprinted through the dark house, her fingers tracing along the walls until she came to Frankie's old bedroom. She flicked on the light switch and gasped. Her son was bound to the metal poles of his bunk bed with thick pieces of rope. He squinted through the harshness of the light.

"Mum?" he croaked, and Katy skidded to her knees, wrapping her arms around him.

"I'm here, sweetie." She cupped her hands around his small, tear-stained face and kissed his forehead. "You're safe now."

Wrestling with the coils of rope, Katy pulled Frankie's arms free from the constraints. She hushed his cries while quickly examining his face and body for any injuries. Satisfied her son's cries were from fear and not physical wounds, she once again scooped him up into her arms and left his bedroom. She crept along the hallway to the front door and pulled down the latch to open it. It wouldn't budge. Katy peered down, but there were no keys in the lock.

"You won't leave me again!" Pete's voice boomed behind her.

Katy turned to face the man and Frankie's arms choked her as they snaked across her neck. She gripped him tightly, hoping he'd understand without words that she wouldn't let him go. Pete lit up the house and she saw the wildness in his eyes. And the knife in his hand.

CHAPTER TWENTY-SEVEN

Once the team had regrouped in a briefing room down the hall, Hamilton instructed Fraser and Clarke to confirm the details they had uncovered for Pete Campbell. Information from the DVLA's records and his current employer, Mr Harvey, verified the suspect's last known address was in Stratford.

"Ask PC Lakhani to liaise with the patrons in The Tavern," Hamilton said, delegating Rocky with the duty of communicating with his Welwyn colleagues. "I'm sure they'll be able to confirm which taxi company Katy Royal used."

With his MIT colleagues occupied, Hamilton ensured the Armed Response Officers were up to speed with their impending strategy and suspect. Planned armed response vehicles would accompany his team to Campbell's address, with SCO19 also on standby. However, with Stratford just under an hour's drive from the station in Charing Cross, Hamilton needed to determine if the man had a second address. Convincing DCI Allen not to distribute Campbell's image to the press had not been easy, but Hamilton knew the element of surprise was paramount. The last thing he wanted was for them to strike at the wrong home and damage Katy and Frankie Royal's chances of being rescued.

The task of apprehending the suspect, who could potentially harm a vulnerable child, enticed painful memories of his daughter. Growing up, Maggie had been a sensitive child, more likely to save a stray cat than to make a new friend, and she'd cry at any Christmas advert with emotional music. He wondered if he had encouraged her to have a stronger character, if he had forced her to stop crying at the little things in life, would the bullies have preyed on her less? *People are always finding new ways to hurt each other; it's what they're good at.*

"Gov!" Clarke yelled, wrenching Hamilton from his reflections. "Pete Campbell of Rose Avenue in Stratford was cautioned five years ago, after a complaint from ex-girlfriend, Rita Bishop. No DNA sample was taken or follow-up investigation. We're trying to get hold of her now."

"What was the caution?"

Clarke flicked through a thin folder and read from the notes, "Rita Bishop called police from Westfield Shopping Centre claiming the suspect was stalking her. He admitted it, saying it was the first time, and signed an on the spot statement that he wouldn't do it again."

"It would have taken a minimum of three complaints from Miss Bishop to the station before they could do anything to help." Hamilton sighed heavily.

Disconnecting a call, Fraser spoke to the room. "That was Mrs Bishop, Rita's mother. Five years ago, her daughter changed her name and moved to France. She confided in her mother that Pete Campbell was aggressive, strangling her to near death during sexual intercourse. When she ended the relationship, he began stalking her and sending dead flowers to her home."

"So, she emigrated to escape him?" Hamilton stated.

Fraser nodded. "After the altercation in the shopping centre, Rita Bishop had no faith in the police because there was no proof the *gifts* were from him, and the force couldn't act. She believed Pete Campbell was going to kill her. Mrs Bishop refused to give me any other information... said we'd have to arrest her before she divulged her daughter's whereabouts."

"I'd prefer to arrest Campbell from what I've heard so far."

"I had a thought about what the owner of the hairdressers said, and asked Mrs Bishop if she could describe our suspect." Fraser paused.

"Let me guess, shaven head, clean face and muscles?"

She clicked her fingers. "You got it, boss."

Hamilton's hand roamed over the sheets of information on the table in front of him. He scooped up the DVLA records for Pete Campbell.

"Well, our suspect is no fool. His driving licence was updated five months ago, with an image of him looking somewhat... shaggy, full beard and long dark hair. How much notice do people take of their taxi drivers?"

"I do, boss, but then it's in my nature to. Do any of us ever really shut down when we leave the station?" Fraser asked.

"No, I don't suppose we do. But, ordinary people, busy getting from one place to the next? Worrying about their jobs, their families and what they're having for dinner; could they give us a description of the cabbie who drove them from the bar to their home last month?"

"Plus, with the car and driver recognition information on the app, which is now used by so many companies, including Embassy Taxis..."

"Pete Campbell would have had to change his appearance in case Katy Royal recognised him from London," Hamilton finished.

He formed a picture of the suspect in his mind and it lead to one place – a place of certainty. Katy and Frankie had been kidnapped from the hospital by their regular taxi driver. With the appeal quiet, he only hoped his team hadn't found their murderer too late.

"Sir, I've just had a word with PC Lakhani," Rocky said. "The Tavern only use one taxi company, so it was easy to track down who hired Pete Campbell. It's a local firm, with no trending technology. Anyway, the owner said Campbell gave him a story about moving to Welwyn with his wife and child, and was in the process of looking for a property."

"Did he give us an address?"

"That's the thing... Campbell supplied him with the address of a Premier Inn when he accepted the job, and hasn't changed it since. Apparently, his *wife* hadn't found their forever home yet."

"What else do we know about Campbell's address in Stratford?"

"He owns it, gov," Clarke said. "He was the sole beneficiary of his father's estate. Campbell's an only child, the mother died when he was young, and he received the house and a dry-cleaning business, the latter of which he sold in 2012."

Hamilton considered the suspect's story, and all the facts they'd uncovered in the last hour. It was time to make a decision. Although he didn't know if the Royals were still alive, he clung to hope.

"The other crime scenes have focused on an element of intimacy, taking place in the women's beds. The attacker wouldn't change tactics and use a hotel. This is personal," Hamilton mused aloud. "But, as a precaution I want PC Lakhani to check it out for us. Rocky, get them to do a recce of the room Campbell used at the Premier Inn. Clarke, get in touch with Stratford. I want the station briefed of our arrival and alerted for back-up if need be. The rest of you, time to make your way to the vehicles. I want blues on until we're within a one-mile radius of Pete Campbell's home address, and then silence. At this time of night, we should be able to get there within half an hour. Let's just hope we're not too late."

CHAPTER TWENTY-EIGHT

"Mummy!" Frankie screamed as he fell to the floor. Pete yanked a handful of Katy's hair and dragged her along the hallway. She gripped her son's hand, as he shuffled on his knees behind her.

"Please, stop this!" she yelled.

Finding herself returned to Frankie's room, a mixture of anger and desperation boiled inside Katy. Hot tears fell silently down her cheeks, prompted more from wrath than fear. How could this man enter her home and terrify her son? When he finally released his hold on her, Katy grabbed her son's large electronic raptor robot and swung it into Pete's face.

"Run, Frankie! Into your old hideout," Katy screamed, repeating herself when the boy hesitated for a few seconds.

The toy had only stunned Pete, yet with her son safely out of the room, the adrenalin surged through Katy's body. She darted away on the balls of her feet, but he was faster, punching her in the face. Katy dropped to the floor, her vision blurred, and she yelped as Pete grabbed her arms and heaved her on top of Frankie's lower bunk bed.

"You bitch," he roared. "I thought you loved me."

"I don't know you," Katy screamed.

Pete flinched. Stepping back a few inches, he retrieved the knife from the floor. Light shone in from the hall, but Katy's left eye was already refusing to open from the assault.

"I thought we had something special. That night... that night we spent together."

"No! You've got it wro –"

The force of Pete's kick crashed into Katy's ribcage before she could finish the sentence. She fell sideways onto the bed, struggling to breathe. He dropped down onto his knees with tears glistening in his eyes.

"I never wanted to hurt you, Katy. Why are you making me do this to you?" he said, and brushed the hair off her face. "I much preferred you with dark hair… I've even bought you the hair dye to help you change back to who you were. But… but, this rejection!"

Pete shook his head repeatedly, bringing the knife into her restricted eye line as he did so. He ran a finger slowly over the blade and stared coldly into her eyes.

"So much has happened. I, I, I forget things… important things…" she whispered.

"A lot has happened. You left me for that monster; you married him and I couldn't find you and, and…"

"Tell me about the night we met," Katy whispered.

Pete dropped back onto his heels and smiled, his eyes glazed as he relived the memory.

"You walked into The Swan on a Friday night, and I knew the minute I saw you we'd be together forever. There was another woman with you, but she was no friend… she left you the moment she'd scored the drugs. That's when I asked if I could buy you a drink, and then you smiled… wow! Adele's song played over and over and we sang, and laughed and danced. That was five years ago, Katy."

She attempted to concentrate on images of places and people's faces flashing through her mind, but it was no help. She couldn't conjure up any memory that corroborated what the man in front of her was saying. He continued talking about them dancing and drinking through the night and, as he did, he released the knife onto the floor. She remained quiet, listening and waiting for an opportunity.

"You saved me that night. My father was dead and Rita had left me. That bitch actually called the cops on me, like I was some kind of criminal. I was in The Swan having a pint trying to calm myself down. I had planned to leave as soon as I'd finished and visit Rita, explain myself, and tell her I loved her. But then you… you came into my life and I realised what love really was. That night in my bedroom, you gave yourself to me… you let me do things to you that proved you were mine. Then you left me too!" Pete bellowed, and he sat forward.

Sliding his fingers around Katy's neck, he pressed his thumbs in the centre. The pressure cutting off her air supply.

"When I found you again, and saw you'd had a child, I didn't know what to think… what to do. It may have been fear that led you to run away from me before and I didn't want that to happen again. So, I've been watching you and waiting… But for what? For you to just leave me again? For you to reject me like the others? No. Fucking. Way."

Katy scrabbled at Pete's hands with her own, desperately trying to pull them away. The shattering pain through her side kept her movements restricted. Just as she gasped for breath, with the darkness closing in on her, she caught sight of a figure standing in the doorway.

CHAPTER TWENTY-NINE

With the vehicles and officers in position, Hamilton assessed the area. Pete Campbell's home was situated in a quiet cul-de-sac, with an abundance of tall trees, window flower boxes and immaculate front gardens. It was a far cry from the busy residential streets of London, an observation that unnerved Hamilton. Their car was parked outside number 79, the detached house furthest down the street, which showed no sign of life inside. Hamilton gave the order and the team made their advance on the property.

Their arrival had stirred interest and, as he banged on the front door, two neighbours stepped out to watch the scene unfold. Silent sirens illumined the street in a tornado of flashing blue and white lights. Radio communication from various points outside Campbell's house blasted through the neighbourhood.

"Sir, the back door is unlocked," Rocky called from the side path.

He followed the officers into the cluttered kitchen, and was greeted by unwashed cutlery and dusty work surfaces. The smell of mould struck him hard and Hamilton clamped his jaw shut, swearing to himself, and swiftly retreating. The team continued searching each room of the house. Each one empty. On the patio, he lifted his head to the dark sky and groaned. Somewhere in the distance, metal clattered and he shone his torch around, following its beam to a large, wooden shed at the far end of the garden.

"Get me something to open this lock," Hamilton shouted.

Within minutes, a uniformed officer had made light work of the padlock with a pair of bolt cutters, and the door swung open. Hamilton pulled a cord, flooding the area with light, and came face-to-face with a horrifying discovery. The old tool shed was more of a lair. He instructed the officer to inform the forensic team and called out to his colleagues as they exited Campbell's home. Clarke whistled as he stepped inside the shed. The four of them stood uncomfortably in the space, studying the walls and work space.

"Campbell's been stalking our victims for some time," Hamilton broke the silence, and examined one wall in particular. "I'd say years for Katy Royal, as her son is still in a pushchair in this photograph. There she is leaving the hairdresser's, images of her as a blonde and brunette, and then exiting The Tavern."

"Have a look at this, sir," Rocky said.

"What is it?"

"Bunch of blank keys and a Dremel multi-tool."

Hamilton scanned the printouts attached to the corkboard above the workstation. They depicted step-by-step instructions of how to copy a key using just a camera, printer and Dremel. Images from Google Earth of Scarlett Mitchell and Emma Jones's properties sat alongside another two unknown houses.

Fraser visibly shuddered. "Is it really that simple to copy keys?"

"Do we know who owns or lives in these two properties?" Hamilton asked, bypassing his colleague's question.

Rocky pointed to one picture. "That's Welwyn, Katy Royal's address. I'm not sure about the other one."

Hamilton slowly gazed around the room while his colleagues discussed how Campbell had entered the victims' buildings. Some of the photographs focused on the women with their sons, some captured them enjoying a lunch out, or playing in the park. But, the majority portrayed them near their homes. He spun back to the workstation and thought of Brad Royal's last words to them.

"She's probably gone home…"

"What's that, gov?" Clarke asked.

"Katy Royal… she is at home. In London." Hamilton yelled his orders as he raced from the garden, back along the side entrance and onto the now crowded street. "Get units to this

London address straightaway, and tell them we're on our way. Clarke, I'll drive."

Hamilton flipped on the sirens and sped away from the nosey neighbours. Fraser and Rocky tailed close behind. Once Clarke had ended the call to Charing Cross station, he turned to his partner.

"Gov, how do you know it's Katy and Brad Royal's place? There's no co-ordinates or other details on the printouts."

"No, but a picture paints a thousand words, and when you know London like I do… Look, it's Bayswater Road, alright." He turned briefly to see Clarke's confused expression. "Every Sunday, come rain or shine, the Royal Park railings are decorated with paintings. Artists come from all over the country to hang their work. Google Earth obviously snapped their shot of the road on a weekend."

Clarke snorted. "Have to say, I never realised you were so cultured, gov."

"I'm not, but the wife is."

Hamilton concentrated on the road, pushing the accelerator as far as safely possible, occasionally inching it further down in deserted areas. A down pouring of guilt flooded him. He'd made the wrong decision sending the teams to Campbell's home, and the hope he'd clung to so tightly began to slip away.

CHAPTER THIRTY

Matthew slipped into the bedroom unnoticed and reached for the silver moneybox on the shelf. Struggling through his own pain, he lifted the heavy object into the air and took a step forward. The ancient floorboards creaked under his weight and the attacker, who now resembled a deranged alopecia patient, released his chokehold on Katy and spun around. Instinctively, Matthew walloped the keepsake down and across the man's skull. Pete slumped forward under the crushing blow, and blood poured from a dark patch of badly shaven hair. Matthew dragged the man to the floor and scooped Katy's limp body into his trembling arms, calling her name over and over again. He lowered his ear to her mouth, desperate to feel the warmth of her breath.

As a child, Matthew had discovered his mother's body knocked out from the brutal force of his father's fist more than once. It had prompted him to enrol in an introductory course to first aid at the age of thirteen; a month later it helped him save his mother's life after she'd been strangled.

Visions of the elderly woman on her deathbed returned to him now and, for the first time in a long time, he felt compelled to save another person's life.

Matthew tipped Katy's head back and pressed against her nose with his thumb and forefinger. He inhaled and lowered his mouth to hers, slowly exhaling and counting to five, then he stopped, repeated the action and reassessed Katy's condition. Ignoring the mumbling groans from behind, he continued. Moments later, he was stunned when a fist connected with his jaw and knocked him backwards.

"She's mine!" the crazed kidnapper roared. "And for that, you will watch her die."

Pinned to the floor, Matthew was dazed, the blows coming hard and fast down into his ribcage; left and right, left and right. He cried out, the pain of his previous injuries awoken by the new attack. Blood trickled down his throat.

"Pete! Stop, please!" Katy's tiny voice shrilled between croaky coughs.

A wave of relief washed over Matthew. As the thug's attention moved to his face, and Pete's knuckles pummelled down, Matthew threw his head sideways and missed the jab. The moment of confusion gave him a chance to retaliate, and he threw his arms up, grabbed Pete and forced the man off his chest. Katy's stifled cries wailed behind them like a theme tune to a movie, and Matthew knew he had to stop this man before he attacked her again. He reciprocated the attack and landed punches into Pete's face until blood oozed from the monster's mouth and nose. Pete's head flopped from side to side like a ragdoll with every strike.

Katy gently pulled back on his shoulder. "Matthew, Matthew... you need to stop."

He clambered off Pete and a stinging agony torched his body. He not only tasted blood, but he could smell it too. Matthew managed to stand, half-bent, but had to stop and rest before moving any further. The urge to wrap his arms around Katy, and explain what he had done, was overwhelming. Yet, his body didn't respond to the messages his brain sent.

"Katy... I..."

"Matthew, I'm sorry, I have to leave you. Frankie is –"

"He's fine! I told him to get out."

"What?" she screamed, and turned to leave the room.

He held her arm weakly. "He helped untie me from the chair and I told him to go and find help."

Katy's ocean blue eyes widened, her already pale face dropped another shade closer to transparent.

"No. No. No. He's hiding... he has a special hiding place in my bedroom... I told him," she said.

Matthew winced as his body straightened. Katy tucked her arm around his waist for support and led him into the hallway. He knew he had to get her out of the house, but he wondered if he truly had the strength to do it.

"I'm sorry, Katy. The keys were in the living room. Frankie didn't want to leave you, but I explained it was the only way he could help you. I insisted he go and knock on a neighbour's house and call the police. Come on, he can't have gone too far. We'll find him together."

She looked around the house, visibly confused and unsure. But, when Matthew reached out and opened the front door with ease, Katy quickly hobbled outside with him onto the street.

The shadows of the night camouflaged their inability to move, and together they froze in the middle of the road. He wanted to ask questions about Pete, and understand why he had been dragged into this nightmare, but he could see Katy's thoughts were elsewhere.

The wind whistled through the trees, blowing around their weak bodies. It seemed to spur Katy on. She dropped her arm from his waist and frantically spun in a circle, wildly searching through the darkness. Matthew knew now was not the time for explanations.

"Let's start looking," he said. "Frankie's bound to be in one of these houses."

Matthew crossed the road to the adjacent front door but Katy stood firm, calling Frankie's name over and over until her scream became a mere cry. Lights flickered on in different homes, with neighbours standing at the windows, twitching their curtains, and then a front door finally opened.

"Is he here? Is my son in there?" Katy ran past Matthew on the driveway and shouted into the face of a large, stocky man.

"Is who here, love?"

"My son. Frankie."

"No. Are you okay? Shall I call the police?"

Matthew stepped between them. "Yes, please call the police."

Katy ignored the man and returned to the pathway, gazing up and down the street.

"We've been attacked… in that house over there," Matthew continued, pointing in the direction behind him. "We'll need an ambulance too."

"No problem! Look, mate, I'll leave the door open for you while I go back in and grab my phone. I suggest you get her inside, she looks awful. You don't look too good yourself."

"Thanks, I appreciate your help."

Matthew thought back to the time he'd wandered away from his mother in Waitrose. He'd only been six or seven, and was bored of waiting at the meat counter, where his mother was requesting freshly cut slices of cured ham for her husband. Matthew had been lured by the thought of sweets and chocolates a few aisles away. He had toddled off, relishing in the choice on offer. A few moments later, the stomach-turning shriek of his name filled the large supermarket. He ran back to his mother to find her pacing the floor, unsure which direction to take to find her son, until her eyes landed on Matthew and she fell to her knees sobbing. His mother had never held him so tight in public, and he realised the few minutes he'd been gone had felt like hours to his mother. After that, she rarely let go of his hand when they were out shopping.

Matthew walked to the kerb, stopped and clutched his aching ribs. He imagined there was nothing more Katy wanted right now than for her son to pop out from behind the bushes of a neighbouring home and yell, '*here I am.*' Indebted to Frankie for rescuing him from the restraints of the rope, Matthew needed to repay the favour and reunite mother and son. He scanned the street and, although curiosity was winning and people were opening their front doors, he couldn't spot Katy.

The throbbing sensation in his temples increased as he tried to decipher the fuzzy memories of when and how he was attacked. His eyes fell on the building he'd escaped from, with its sparkling white bay windows and glossed front door. From the outside, it was easy to believe it was a perfect home for a perfect family. Just as his own home had once looked. Undecided if he could be drawn into another hostile family life, Matthew hesitated. But, regardless of what his mind thought, he was inexplicable drawn to Katy Royal.

A dark figure in Frankie's bedroom window caught his attention. His body stiffened at the thought of the strange man's bloodstained body lying on the floor. He spun around, searching again for Katy or Frankie. He was alone. Matthew focused on the house again but he was too late, the net curtain of the boy's room fell slowly back into place, concealing his view of inside the house.

Another shadow moved swiftly across the living room. Matthew stepped closer, but an explosion of glass knocked him flying back. He clamped his eyes shut and covered his head, a ringing noise shattering his eardrums. Finding the strength to pull himself up, Matthew sat on the ground and watched the clouds of smoke and dancing flames scorch the front of the house.

Matthew ignored the pain and crawled closer to the open front door, towards the radiating fire, driven onwards by a tremendous urge to protect the mother and her son from this violent man. He contemplated whether or not Katy had returned to the house, impelled by her doubt of Frankie's escape, or if indeed their attacker had dragged her back into the building while Matthew wasn't paying attention.

Sirens rang out in the distance, their distinctive danger signal growing closer and closer. Voices of concern and caution shrieked in the background, but Matthew understood nothing. His surroundings became a fog of chaos. He blocked it out and, seeing only Katy's beautiful face and hearing only her son's sweet voice, he knew he had to save them.

CHAPTER THIRTY-ONE

Hamilton slammed his foot on the brake, coming to an emergency halt at the entrance of Bayswater Road. Screams and sirens mingled together, as onlookers gathered in their nightwear to watch those running from the homes either side of the spreading fire. Checking the address, he realised it was the home of Katy and Brad Royal, and sprinted down the street. The descending full moon illuminated the horror etched on the faces of the people as he pushed them further away from the flames. Clarke, Fraser and Rocky created a perimeter around the maisonette, ensuring every civilian stood behind the barrier, and squad cars arrived from various directions. Hamilton jogged over to the nearest uniformed officer.

"I'm Detective Inspector Hamilton. Do we know what's going on?"

"No, not quite, sir. We were called by one of the neighbours for an alleged attack and, while he was on the phone, he informed the operator of the fire."

"Fire brigade and ambulance en route?"

"Of course, sir. ETA is five minutes."

The young man adjusted his hat and rushed past Hamilton to help his team with the crowd control. As had become the norm, people stood amidst a tragedy with their phones primed. They shouted and demanded answers he couldn't give them. Katy's name was repeatedly called out and the fear he'd arrived too late smacked him across the face.

"You can't go in there!" yelled the uniformed officer. "No!"

Hamilton spun around and watched a wounded man run through the front door, swallowed by the black smoke. The living room window ledge fell to the ground, exposing the house with another blast of fire. Renewed cries erupted from the assembled crowd; they flinched and shifted backwards. Hamilton leapt through the barrier, shed himself of his long, tailored coat and ran into the house.

The fire was contained, trapped behind the living room door. But the thick smoke choked him and his eyes watered instantly. Hamilton dipped his head, coughed and swung his arm over his face, protecting himself as much as possible. His fingers trailed along the wall as he walked further into the burning home.

He peered into the first room on the left. It was difficult to see clearly, but easy to assume it was a child's bedroom. His chest tightened at the thought of Frankie, but he was distracted by a horrifying wail resonating through the house. He followed the cries of a banshee, walking past the living room door. He flinched at the distant heat as it attacked his skin, and the sound of wood as it popped and sizzled under the weight of the flames. The front door was in his eyeline, a mere five feet away, and a breeze of fresh air drifted through the entrance. Hamilton took a deep, muffled breath, pulled his arm closer across his mouth and ploughed on along his path. He slowly pushed open a door, and the howls and protests grew stronger and louder.

"Let me go!" a woman objected.

The room was barely lit by a small lamp, and the smoke had begun its journey inside. The unidentified male gripped Katy Royal by the arms and yanked her around the room. Despite the cosmetic change, Hamilton recognised the woman from the photographs in the incident room.

"Katy... my name is Detective Inspector Hamilton. I'm here to help." His eyes remained on the bruised man's face, eager to study the reaction his arrival prompted.

"Frankie! Frankie!" she continued to cry.

The man faced Hamilton, without releasing his hold of Katy. "Help me, please... I'm trying to get her out..."

Hamilton raised his hand to stop the man coming any further. Katy thrashed around on the floor calling her son's name, straining herself in an attempt to break free. The inferno whistled around them.

"Sir, who are you?"

"Matthew Webb. A friend of Katy's. I was taken by that madman too. Please!"

Hamilton registered the man's speedy response and believed him; it really wasn't the time to dither. He rushed to the man's side, placed his hands under Katy and helped haul her onto her feet.

"Please… Please! My son, he's in the house!"

"No, Katy, listen to me! He got out before us," Matthew said.

While the man's authoritative voice was convincing, Hamilton understood why Katy was reluctant to leave her home. It's a parent's duty to guarantee their child's safety, a job that comes with no instructions. But, in challenging times, an overwhelming instinct is ignited. Hamilton sensed that parental reflex, as strongly as the failure he suffered.

"Katy, we will find your son, I *promise* you that," he uttered in her ear. "But we'll be no use to him if we do not get out of this house now."

She finally stopped resisting and looked up at Hamilton. Her red, swollen eyes stared into his for a few moments and her breathing steadied. He wondered if the scars of unspeakable loss were visible to another parent in turmoil. If they were, she didn't comment. Silently, she nodded her head and used the two men as crutches to lead her from the bedroom.

The hallway was full of commotion. Flashlights shone in Hamilton's eyes, instructions were yelled through the smoke, and flashes of yellow from the firefighters' protective uniforms became a beacon to follow. Hamilton freed Katy's arms, and allowed Matthew and the firefighter to escort her out of the front door. He stood adjacent to the smaller bedroom and moved to cross over the doorway.

"Sir! Out of here immediately," a firefighter called, pulling him back into the hallway.

"There could be a child in there... I didn't look..."

"That's our job, sir. Now, please."

The firefighter's large hands gripped onto his shoulder, communicating to Hamilton that he had no choice but to do as commanded. Half-heartedly, he allowed himself to be pushed along the hall, the clean night-air enticed him further; when suddenly he was hurled through the front door. He crashed down onto the pavement, the heaviness of the firefighter's weight on his back, his head ricocheting off the ground.

CHAPTER THIRTY-TWO

Unfamiliar hands and metal implements brushed against Hamilton's skin as he regained consciousness in the back of the ambulance. He pushed away the paramedic, mumbled an apology and sat up. Clarke stood at the open van doors with his back to him, and Hamilton was relieved to see they were stationary on Bayswater Road. Before anyone prevented him, Hamilton was off the stretcher, down the steps and by his partner's side. He called back to the paramedic, instructing she give her time to someone who required the assistance more.

"Gov, that's not a great idea. Let her give you a full examination," Clarke said with a wink.

"I'm fine! A knock on the head is all. How's the firefighter?"

"Your human shield, you mean? Absolutely fine, he got the two of you out of there just in time. His colleagues are inside the property controlling the blaze now."

"What about Katy and…"

"Matthew Webb? They're in the second ambulance across the road getting checked out. They both suffered smoke inhalation, but seem okay. Not sure about their previous injuries as yet. Fraser and Rocky are staying near the house to see if anyone else is rescued."

"Come with me, Clarke. I want to have a chat with Katy and find out what the hell happened in that house, and more about Pete Campbell."

Hamilton coughed, flinching at the unwelcoming pain the movement brought, and lightly touched the tingling swelling on his forehead.

"What do you think you were playing at, gov? Running into the fire like that... I was scared to death," Clarke confessed as they strolled down the street.

"I wasn't really thinking of anything. I just reacted."

"Well, maybe next time you could think of your wife. Things could have ended very differently if that firefighter hadn't pushed you out. It would have been me knocking on your front door, telling Elizabeth you'd never be home for dinner again."

Hamilton detected the severity in his partner's tone and refrained from answering with a sarcastic response. Unusual for Clarke to adopt the scolding persona, Hamilton thought, but understood the seriousness of the lecture. He nodded and patted Clarke on the back. It was a scene he hoped his partner never had to enact, and a message his wife wouldn't have to suffer in the near future. She was vulnerable enough at the moment, he thought.

The sun made its ascent on a new day over London, brightening a residential road filled with uncertainty and secrecy. The blaze was almost controlled, and the neighbours had filtered away as the lamp posts automatically switched off. Katy sat on the steps of the ambulance and took no interest in Hamilton. Her skin had been darkened by the smoke and eyes glazed with sadness. Two paramedics busied with Matthew inside the van, while one man concentrated on the shell of a woman in front of him.

When Hamilton finally grabbed Katy's attention, she offloaded everything she had endured since accepting the taxi from the hospital in Welwyn, and how Pete had revealed himself and that her son was still missing.

"Clarke, can you get Fraser and Rocky to canvas the area. This road was swarming with people, someone must have seen a small boy. Remember, he used to live here so most of them will know him. Tell them to check inside their houses if need be." Hamilton moved closer and whispered in his partner's ear. "Then I want you to stay with the fire crew. I want to know the minute they find a body in that house."

Clarke raced off and Hamilton crouched, perching himself on the kerb next to Katy. A whirlwind of white noise encircled them and she glared at her fingers, nervously twiddling a piece of tissue.

"So, you knew Pete Campbell?" he asked.

"Yes. No." She sighed. "I don't really know. Pete was my taxi driver since I started working at The Tavern. Tonight, when he shaved himself… I recognised him as the taxi driver I sometimes used in London. His name was Peter. I didn't take any notice of him, not even the name." She wiped the tears trickling down her cheeks and inhaled a deep breath. "I have to find my son…"

"Katy, I have to tell you, Pete Campbell has a personal collection of photos of you and your son… and four other victims. You're lucky to have escaped tonight."

"Lucky!" she shrieked. "I have no idea where my son is. Don't you understand? How can you call me the damn lucky one!"

Hamilton accepted her anger, nodding in agreement to the woman. "Once the firefighters have assessed the house, we'll have a better understanding of what exactly is going on here. But, other than in the capacity of driver and customer, did you know Pete?"

"The man's crazy. He kept saying we'd met before."

"And had you?"

"No… I don't know. He mentioned some pub, The Swan… no, I don't remember." Katy shoved the tissue in her pocket and scrambled up. "I have to get to my son."

Hamilton stood and took her shaking hand in his. "Katy, listen to me. My team and the firefighters are looking for Pete and your son right now, as we're speaking. Let them do their jobs. I'm sure the paramedics will want you and Matthew to get checked out at the hospital –"

"Not without my son!" she yelled, and yanked her hand away.

"Okay, but please, just wait here for now. I'll send a uniformed officer to sit with you and take an official statement."

Katy crumbled, falling to the step again. Fresh tears replaced old and she sobbed with her head in her hands. Hamilton briefly spoke with the female paramedic who informed him Matthew's injuries concerned her more than Katy's. Between the two of them there were broken ribs and cheekbone, swelling and loss of blood, however, both were refusing hospital treatment. Hamilton requested the paramedic stay on the scene until the house had been safely cleared; he also wanted another pair of eyes on Katy, unsure of her mental state.

Clarke beckoned him over with the wave of his hand. Once regrouped outside the house, his partner explained the firefighters had contained the inferno.

"They're doing a final check now, but their chief is confident there is no one in that building."

Hamilton frowned. "Adult or child?"

"No. There is absolutely no trace of anyone in there." Clarke raised his eyebrows. "They've said it was clearly an arson attack, with petrol in the far side of the living room. It seems the door was then pulled shut before the arsonist left."

"Katy's adamant she saw Pete Campbell at her son's window. Paranoid her son didn't escape, she entered the house, but she didn't comment as to whether that was before or after the fire started."

Clarke shrugged. "You know, our minds can play tricks on us. With everything that woman's been through in the last twenty-four hours, who's to say what she really saw… or if the timeline of her events is accurate?"

Hamilton and Clarke walked away from the house and back down the street towards the other half of their team, and the various additional officers who had arrived in the last few hours. Their presence attracted new interest with commuters passing by; although eager as they were to get to the nearest train station or bus stop, they slowed down with an inquisitive desire. So many faces had come and gone in the last few hours, Hamilton wondered if they had really let the suspect slip by them so easily.

"Bad news, boss," Fraser said, when they met by his car. "No one has seen Frankie and he didn't knock on any of the closer homes."

"Right…" Hamilton rubbed his ever-growing aching temple. "We can't assume Pete Campbell has kidnapped the boy, because by all accounts Frankie fled before anyone else. But, let's get both of their faces out into the public domain immediately. Get uniform to appeal to the neighbours again, this time with images and details of Campbell's car. It might jog someone's memory. I'll get in contact with the chief and request he gives the media a heads-up of a high-alert missing child… although he could have just run off into the night, scared and alone. Okay, I also want you to ask the officers to request volunteers so we can conduct a sweep of the local vicinity. Fraser, get back to the station and dig deeper on Campbell. Comb through the evidence we found in his garden shed. I want to know everything you can find on him; it might give us a clue to where he's gone."

"We'll have the local hospitals checked too," Clarke added. "Matthew Webb explained he gave Campbell a good beating in return and knocked the man unconscious twice. Well, that's what he thought. Either way, he might need medical attention."

Rocky whistled. "Knocked him out twice? Christ, who is this Pete Campbell guy, Robocop?"

Hamilton ignored the playful comment and spoke firmly. "We're dealing with a violent man who outwardly appears to be a non-threatening, normal member of society. He's had the ability to blend in and hide in plain sight for months, years even! To me, that makes him a very dangerous and frightening man, who has already murdered four people, and brought Katy and Frankie Royal here to do the same. Not to mention the out of character addition of abducting Matthew Webb. Pete Campbell's plan was clearly interrupted. Who knows what direction he may take now, especially if he has kidnapped the boy? Frankie's life may be held in the balance, at the whim of a madman. Pete Campbell will most certainly be vexed that months of formulating his plans have now been ruined. So, for now, let's have some protection on Katy Royal, as he may come back for her. Most importantly, let's find this lunatic!"

Although he trusted his partner, Hamilton decided to speak to the chief firefighter himself. He needed to hear the information first-hand, because only he had seen the look of conviction in Katy's eyes when she'd explained someone was in her house after the explosion. He spun around and came face-to-face with the woman.

"Sorry to startle you, Inspector."

"Is everything okay?" he asked, looking over her shoulder at the closing doors of the ambulance.

"The pain is too much for Matthew, so he's decided to go to the hospital. Do you think I could sit in one of the cars?" Katy asked.

"Of course, yes."

He turned back and called out for Rocky's attention. Pointing to his colleague, he told Katy to wait in his vehicle until he returned to update her. The woman resembled a zombie as she shuffled away from him. Hamilton recognised her pain. Whether or not he would deliver life-changing, devastating news, it remained his duty to find out what had happened to her son.

CHAPTER THIRTY-THREE

The handsome officer, Katy now knew as Rocky, opened the rear car door and smiled at her. Although it was an unmarked vehicle, she wondered if the locks would restrict her from escaping. Too many cop shows on the television had planted that particular seed in her mind.

"I'm not under arrest, am I?" she attempted to giggle, and hated herself for doing so.

"No. I guess you can sit up front," he replied, closing one door and opening another.

"Thanks... do you think it will take us long to get to Hertfordshire?" Rocky frowned and remained quiet. Katy licked her dry lips. "Erm... DI Hamilton said you'd drive me to my flat in Welwyn."

Her stomach clenched as the officer turned in the direction his boss had been standing in moments before. Luckily, Hamilton appeared to be out of hearing range, and Rocky returned his attention to Katy.

"That's why he called you over," she continued. "They've taken my friend to the hospital and I need to get cleaned up. I said I'd report to the station in Welwyn straight after."

"Ah, I see," Rocky finally said. "No bother at all, jump in, Mrs Royal."

She dipped her head, climbed in the car and sat in the passenger's seat. Her sweaty palms slipped on the door handle and a burning heat flushed against her cheeks. Katy asked the officer to call her by her first name while gazing out of the window, silently urging the engine to start without any attention from those in the surrounding area. Thanks to Inspector Hamilton's earlier comment, her plan was now clear. She dismissed the pain scorching through her body and focused on what needed to be done.

Katy exhaled a large sigh of relief as they pulled away from her former home but, as they drove past the red bricked apartments on Old Marylebone Road, she frowned and turned to the officer.

"You haven't asked me for any directions."

"No need, I live in Welwyn so know the best route to take. We should be in town within thirty minutes."

Usually, the Irish twang to his accent and unique name would prompt Katy to ask questions and engage in conversation. Instead, she zoned out as Rocky continued to waffle on about where he lived, and his secondment to the London Met Police. Not counting on actually travelling all the way home, her mind shot into overdrive as she devised a back-up plan. There was no choice now.

"Can I use your phone quickly please?" Katy asked.

"Everything okay?"

She hesitated. "Yes, it's just I have no idea where my belongings are. I have no keys for my apartment and thought I should text my neighbour... she has a spare key."

Rocky's eyes never left the road as he removed one hand from the steering wheel and retrieved the mobile from his inside coat pocket.

"We probably should have checked before we headed off, but I can drive you directly to the station if there's a problem."

"No!" Katy snapped. "I mean, there's no problem. She has kids and... it's still so early. I'm sure they won't have gone out yet."

Rocky turned down his lips and nodded, his fingers rhythmically drumming on the steering wheel to the hushed musical tones playing over the radio. Katy was surprised to find the phone had no passcode, but then who would steal a copper's mobile, she thought? Thumbing over the screens, she found the app she wanted and began her search. Her eyes flicked discreetly between the phone and the officer until she had the information she wanted.

"All done, thank you," Katy said, and lowered his mobile into the cup holder compartment.

"We're not too far now, hopefully your neighbour will reply."

"Oh, she did. Yes, she's at home."

"Must have forgotten to switch it off silent. I'm always doing that," Rocky replied, and indicated left to exit the A1 at Hertford.

Katy chewed her bottom lip and stole a glimpse at the uninterested officer. Part of her screamed to confess everything to him; he gave off a relaxed, laid-back impression that the Inspector did not. She wondered if it were possible to trust this man with her secret.

Her husband's possessive personality and Pete's bloodstained face returned to haunt her. She pushed their images aside and focused on the face of the only man she had ever truly trusted, her father.

Born in London, Katy's father had taken advantage of the low property prices in the seventies and built a steady business buying, transforming and selling homes. His flexible work schedule meant Katy spent a lot of time with him during her teenage years, and they always had something to discuss; no more so than their heated disagreements surrounding their love of literature, forged from his days of teaching English. He had married his childhood sweetheart and together they embodied the fairy-tale romance. Cynical of fictional love to begin with, Katy often teased her parents, while secretly hoping one day she'd find a man like her father who wanted to marry her.

"Can you think of anywhere your son may have gone?" Rocky asked, yanking Katy from her reverie.

"What?"

"Well, I'm just thinking, perhaps your son was scared and he decided to go somewhere special to him. Maybe to a place where only his mother would know where to find him."

Katy struggled to hold back the volcano of tears threatening to erupt. "Frankie is only five years old, Officer. It was dark... I can't believe he would run away. He's never done that before. Sadly, it's not the first time he's witnessed a man overpower me."

She caught Rocky's sideward glance before turning back to face the road. Flashing in a haze before her eyes were pedestrians, and the groomed greenery of Welwyn Garden City, all barely seen through her glassy eyes. Katy knew the policeman could never understand the power of a mother's love. What needed to be done could only be fulfilled by her. She was alone.

CHAPTER THIRTY-FOUR

Hamilton clicked his fingers and pointed to the driver's side of the car, while listening to the monotonous dialling tone on his mobile phone. He climbed into the passenger's seat and Clarke took his cue, jumping in behind the wheel.

"Finally! Where the hell are you?" Hamilton roared down the phone as the car cruised out of Bayswater Road.

"I'm still in Welwyn, sir. But I was just about to call you." Rocky replied.

"What are you bloody doing in Welwyn?"

"I drove Katy Royal back to her apartment, as you requested, sir."

"No I did not. The instruction was to sit in the car and *wait*."

"No..." Rocky hesitated. "That's not the message she passed onto me."

Hamilton frowned, the car picking up speed alongside Hyde Park as they drove back to the station; he couldn't understand why Katy had duped a member of his team.

"Anyway, sir, as I was saying, about calling you..."

"What is it, Rocky?"

"I'm currently parked outside Katy Royal's apartment."

"Good, you haven't left."

"No, sir. I thought she was acting a bit suspicious during the drive here. Used my phone to text her neighbour, but must have deleted it because there's no message. She also switched my phone onto silent so I wouldn't hear any notifications. Should I pop up to her flat, or try and find the neighbour?"

"Rocky, do you have a good view of the entrance?" Hamilton asked.

"Yes, sir. I'm hidden away, but I can see the apartment just fine."

"Right, don't move and do not take your eyes off that door, do you understand? I want to know the minute Katy Royal exits that building. There was no way she was leaving London without her son. I want to know what changed her mind so quickly."

"I won't let her out of my sight, sir."

Hamilton ended the call, and although he was certain his partner had picked up the gist of the conversation, he relayed the information back to Clarke. The situation bothered him. He had seen the look of distress in Katy Royal's eyes and wondered what her next move was. He was desperate to get back to the station and exchange updates with Fraser.

"Gov, I'm going to pop down the street to Penny's Bakery," Clarke announced after he cut the engine. "I think we all need some refuelling."

Exhaustion suddenly attacked Hamilton. Although he knew everyone would plough through the fatigue they had all become accustomed to in this job, they needed some sustenance to help the battle. Standing in the courtyard, Hamilton reached into his wallet and handed his partner some money.

"Stock up on refreshments for the office, Clarke. Good thinking. I'll meet you upstairs."

In the incident room, Hamilton marched over to Fraser, busy updating the white evidence boards. He noticed the empty chocolate wrapper and diet coke can by her computer. It wasn't even midday, but he couldn't judge her breakfast choices when not one of them had slept in over twenty-four hours.

"Boss, I'm glad you're back," Fraser said. "I've just this minute got off the phone to Audrey Gibson. She examined the balaclava found in Campbell's shed and it was a match."

"What, to the woollen fibre under Emma Jones's fingernail?"

"Yes, boss."

"Okay… Good." His mind pieced together parts of the puzzle. "Before leaving the scene, the firefighters confirmed no one was in that house. We have no idea where Pete's gone, or if in fact he has Frankie Royal. It's a matter of urgency that we find them both."

"I've checked the local hospitals, but there's no record of Campbell being seen."

"He'd be foolish to use his real name."

"I gave a description, but it was futile. We can't be sure of his appearance now, and the receptionist couldn't check every bed or cubicle."

"No, of course not. Have an officer fax over Campbell's image to all the major hospitals within a five-mile radius. The chief touched base with us before we left Bayswater, he was travelling to an emergency press conference about Frankie Royal. We're hoping it'll be aired in the next hour or so."

He updated Fraser on Rocky's whereabouts and, before they could discuss Katy Royal's actions, Clarke barged through the doors with both hands full – one with a container of pastries, and the other with a tray of hot beverages. Hamilton suggested they all take a break before delving back into the search. Most of them were usually content to eat on the job, so he grabbed a warm sausage roll and polystyrene cup of tea and perched on the table in front of the evidence board. His mind reacted immediately to the fuel, eyes speeding over the images and connections and timelines before him. He grabbed a marker and added a new link between Campbell and Katy Royal.

"What's The Swan, gov?" Clarke asked, joining his boss.

"Just the name of a pub Katy briefly mentioned earlier, but she had no further information about it."

Clarke placed his coffee on the table and retrieved his mobile from his back pocket. After a few minutes, he was reciting the details shown on the phone's screen.

"Right, let's have a look at the map. There is one on Clapham Road, Sudbury, Stratford, Kington –"

"Stop, click on the Stratford one," Hamilton interrupted.

"Okay… The Swan was a public house on Stratford High Street, close to the train station, but it closed in 2013." He paused to glance at Hamilton. "Despite public interest, it was never renovated, reopened or sold. That's in Campbell's area."

"Yes, and apparently, he was adamant that's where the pair first met."

Hamilton peered closer at the information, his index finger drumming on his lips. He reached over the desk and browsed through the records, pulling out the financial information collated.

"In 2012, Campbell sells his father's lucrative local business and then closes that bank account. What did he do with all that cash?" Hamilton asked.

"You think he bought the pub, why?"

"It could be sentimental, if it's the first place he saw Katy. Call the Stratford station and find out if anyone knows anything about this pub, particularly before it was sold, and who owned it."

"That could take ages, and we're not even sure that's where Campbell's money actually went. He could have bought a car, another apartment or probably used it to deck out that dungeon in his back garden. We can't follow a cash trail, gov."

"I know, you're right, Clarke. And it could be a long shot, but that monster mentioned it while he had three people gagged and bound in the Royal's house, so it must be important to him."

His partner complied, and Hamilton sat at the desk surrounding himself with every shred of information they had obtained on Campbell's life so far. He needed to create a vivid image of the murderer's character. By creating a clearer understanding of who Pete Campbell was, there would be a chance he could apprehend the suspect before another innocent life was stolen.

"Boss, the incident room just received a call about a robbery at a chemist," Fraser said, interrupting him from the task. "The attending officers scanned the CCTV footage and recognised the thief as Campbell. He stole a variety of strong painkillers and other first aid equipment."

"So, he's planning DIY treatment. Was he alone?"

"Inside the chemist, yes. However, the external camera caught his car parked outside and, although the image isn't clear, there appears to be a small body lying in the back seat."

"He's got Frankie Royal! Where's the chemist located, Fraser?"

"Old Street in Islington."

Hamilton's chair screeched along the floor. He flew to the evidence board and traced his finger along the large map.

"Old Street is the same route we took when we drove to Campbell's house. Damn it! That maniac would have driven straight past this station." Hamilton balled his hands into fists. "Although the chemist is between the Royal household and Stratford, I don't want to make any assumptions this time about where Campbell might be. Fraser, let's first confirm there are sentries in place at Campbell's address, and then put them on high alert. But, I highly doubt he'd return home."

"He might do, boss. How's he to know we've even linked him to Katy Royal yet, let alone already have his home under surveillance?"

"This man is dangerous, but he's not stupid. Press reports are imminent, if not already in the public domain, and the robbery was careless and unplanned, the opposite of how this man has previously acted. I'd say Campbell's aware."

Fraser nodded. "Okay, leave it with me, boss."

"I'll get in touch with the automatic number plate recognition data centre and see if we can evaluate which route Campbell took after he fled the Islington area."

Before Hamilton could make the necessary call, Clarke covered his own phone receiver and explained he'd been put on a hold. Stratford's desk sergeant was in the process of contacting one of the station's longest standing police community support officers.

"Apparently, we can't get better than this woman's local knowledge of Stratford, as she was born and raised in the area," Clarke said. "As well as being a PCSO with the station for ten years."

"Definitely sounds like the contact we need to talk to right now."

Clarke gave him the thumbs up and mouthed that the woman was in the building. Hamilton returned his focus to the office phone but was distracted once again, this time by the ping of his mobile.

He read Rocky's message. "Katy Royal is on the move."

CHAPTER THIRTY-FIVE

Rocky peered through the long, dangling tree branches that danced in the breeze around his windscreen. Two women exited the apartment and hastily climbed into the black Mitsubishi Outlander outside. There was a confidence surrounding Katy Royal, now she had washed and changed into clean jeans and a red parka, her short, blonde hair tied back. He immediately recognised the driver as the upstairs neighbour who had denied knowing Katy during his earlier search of the property with Fraser. Grabbing his mobile, Rocky made a note of the registration plate and sent a brief text to Hamilton. He started the car and followed at a safe distance.

The driver sped along the dual carriageway adjacent to Stanborough Park and the River Lea, switching lanes with no indication. The car circled the next three roundabouts and past the Hertfordshire Constabulary. Rocky had a desire to call his colleagues for back up, but was unsure as to why he was chasing a victim of crime. Knowing the area well, Rocky speculated on their destination. Remaining a few cars behind, travelling along Osborn Way, the Howard Centre came into view and confirmed his instinct. The Outlander came to a screeching halt outside the underpass entrance for Welwyn Garden City railway station and Katy hopped out.

Rocky closed in behind them as the driver sped off and Katy ran inside the station. Grateful for the one remaining space, Rocky swiftly parallel parked and grabbed his coat from the passenger's seat. With Katy now out of sight, he had no choice but to lock the car and leave it abandoned without a parking permit; the last thing he wanted was to dissatisfy Hamilton by losing their victim. He didn't want his first investigation in London to be his last.

He sprinted through the entrance, slowing his pace when he spied a flash of red making its way to the main station ticket office. He quickly picked up a copy of The Metro and hid behind the inky sheets of news. Katy was soon on the move again, towards the platform overshadowed by a train signalling its departure. Reluctantly, Rocky flew along the platform in her wake, hoping he hadn't been spotted. He jumped onto the carriage before the one Katy had chosen, just as the doors slammed shut behind him, and the train jerked into movement. He carefully walked through the coach until he was close enough to observe her through the glass windowed doors.

Katy appeared edgy, fiddling with something in her hands and unable to select a seat. Rocky jumped back from view before her eyes settled in his direction. Satisfied she wasn't about to open the door and cross over into his carriage, Rocky chanced another look, and peered back through the glass. Katy had finally chosen a seat, her head resting on the window as the train glided through the Hatfield and Welham Green's picturesque scenery. He pulled away and, confident he couldn't lose the woman on a moving train, retrieved his mobile phone and called Lakhani.

"Alright, mate," the PC answered.

"Yeah, listen I need you to do something for me," Rocky replied, and brought him up to date with the current situation. "Can you have a word with Katy Royal's neighbour for us? She obviously knows more than she's letting on, and may have some clue as to what Katy's plan is. Find out what you can and let me know."

"Leave it with me," Lakhani said, and ended the call.

The train screeched to a halt at Potters Bar and Rocky ignored the distractions from other passengers and discreetly focused on the red coat. Despite living in Welwyn for a couple of years, Rocky was unfamiliar with the railway service, and therefore unaware of the train's direction of travel. As they pulled away from the station, he waited for a carriage announcement before calling Hamilton.

"Sir, we're headed for Moorgate Underground station," he explained, after his superior demanded information.

"How long will it take?"

Rocky angled his head and concentrated on the railway map. "It's seventeen stops, so I'm not sure… I'd hazard a guess at about forty to fifty minutes. But we have no way of knowing where she'll jump off between here and there."

"No, but I'd bet my badge on Katy returning to the city. We've had a development in the case."

"But why, sir? What's she doing?"

Hamilton huffed loudly. "Unfortunately, we haven't discovered that part out yet, but she's certainly part of something we're trying to understand."

"Wouldn't it be easier if I just approached her?"

"No!" Hamilton snapped. "There's a reason she ran away from us, and confronting her may ruin our chances of understanding why that was. We're closing in on Campbell and have a possible location for him in the Stratford area. I want you to stick with Katy and keep me updated. Don't let me down, son."

"I won't, sir," Rocky said to the emptiness of his iPhone home screen.

He wasn't disheartened his superior had hung up without a farewell; in fact, a sense of relief overwhelmed him. Rocky perceived Hamilton as a man on the edge, like a bubbling pot waiting to overspill, and he didn't want to be the reason for that explosion. He was quickly learning there was little time for pleasantries. The secondment to MIT had welcomed him into one of the most in-depth investigations he'd worked on during his career. So far, he'd only skimmed the surface of the case but, after being handed the baton of responsibility, he was tenacious enough to prove his worth.

CHAPTER THIRTY-SIX

Hamilton jumped onto the nearest computer and securely logged in. He clicked the desktop's Internet Explorer shortcut, his mind racing as fast as his fingers could type the words into the search engine. Within seconds, masses of results filled the monitor and he double-clicked on a London train service map. His eyes scanned the red route highlighting the journey from Welwyn Garden City to Moorgate while his fingers lightly traced over the screen; his home town of famous landmarks and tourist attractions at his fingertip. He waited. Something in the back of his mind slowly clawed its way to the forefront, and then he saw it. Curved upwards on the map, to the right of Moorgate station, he found the Queen Elizabeth Olympic Park signpost.

He swiftly opened a new tab, searched new keywords and waited for the information to load and process. The corners of his mouth turned up, discovering the route Rocky was currently travelling on was due to stop at Highbury and Islington, and would allow a direct connection to Stratford. Hamilton grabbed his mobile from the desk and composed a text message to Rocky, his thumbs dancing across the Samsung Galaxy quicker than ever before. He needed to inform the lad about Katy's destination. At least where his gut feeling told him she was going.

"Right, we're taking two cars and getting over to The Swan pub now," Hamilton ordered Clarke and Fraser. "Granted, we made a mistake storming Campbell's home address and we can't afford to mess up again. But, ANPR has our suspect's vehicle on Stratford High Street an hour ago, if we wait any longer we risk losing him. And Frankie Royal for that matter."

Hamilton's jaw tightened and his exasperation escalated at the thought of failing. At the thought of abandoning an innocent child in the hands of a killer.

"I understand but wait, boss, the back-up teams aren't in play yet," Fraser called after him.

He paused, pushing the door half open, and turned to face his colleague. "I'll be damned if any further harm is going to come to that boy, just because we sat around here and failed to act quickly enough. There's no harm in the three of us going ahead and doing a recce of the location before the other teams arrive."

"Works for me," Clarke said, and breezed by his partner out of the door.

Hamilton raised his eyebrows at Fraser and observed what he thought was a moment of hesitation in her reaction. She quietly nodded, snatched her coat and mobile phone from the desk and joined them.

As it approached midday, Hamilton could barely believe it was less than twenty-four hours since their last journey to Stratford. He used the time to touch base with the local station, who confirmed no one had returned to Campbell's home address, and exchanged text messages with Rocky. If they hadn't been covering such a wide geographical area, he would have sent Fraser to assist the temporary officer. Although Rocky seemed confident in the current role, Hamilton recognised the pressure of inconspicuously following a person of interest. Further difficulty came when doing this on London's transport system. Whether it was the underground or overground, rail or bus, the service embodied a matrix of people scurrying and pushing, clustering together and ignoring others. Katy Royal could easily vanish.

Clarke drove past The Swan and turned onto a side road to park the car. Hamilton glanced out of the window and watched Fraser follow their lead, parking a few spaces ahead of them. The trio retrieved their stab vests from the car boot. Suited up, and ready for the imminent task, Hamilton gave his orders.

"Put your jackets on over your vests, I don't want to attract any attention too early," he said, zipping up his own. "Fraser I want you to stay out on the high street. You're the command centre for when SCO19 arrive and our point of communication with them until they do. Clarke, we'll patrol the perimeter to gauge if anyone is actually inside."

The two men walked briskly around the corner onto Stratford High Street, scanning the vicinity and building of interest. The pub had long since been cared for, and stood out among the boutiques and chain of coffee shops. A busy neighbourhood, which had benefitted from the 2012 Olympic Games, gave The Swan a prime location for trade from the local businesses, campuses and tenants. Hamilton speculated why it had remained vacant for over three years, and as though his partner had read his thoughts, Clarke spoke in a hushed tone.

"That PCSO woman I spoke to, Sumaria was her name, sounded like she knew just about everything that goes on around here. The previous pub owner was a dodgy guy but, regardless of the reputation, they never had any concrete evidence to arrest him with anything. Anyway, Sumaria said he was running it into the ground and jumped at the chance of selling up. He moved out of the town as soon as the money exchanged hands."

"What about contracts and bank details?"

Clarke shrugged. "Okay, so maybe Sumaria didn't have *all* the answers… but she said she'd look into it further. I'd happily talk to her again, gov. But, whoever bought it, paid swiftly and paid with cash. No one's been seen in there since."

As they approached closer to the building, Hamilton eyed its entire exterior. The potential malevolence behind its doors, hidden in plain sight as parents strolled by with pushchairs and workers popped in next door for lunch. He hated to admit it to his partner, but the place made him shudder. It had been a long time since he'd ignored his gut feeling.

"Let's not stop here, those young guys will probably start filming us for Facebook or YouTube in a minute," he murmured to Clarke, eyeing the rowdy teenagers loitering outside Burger King.

"What's the plan?"

"We'll take the side alley. Surely it has to lead to another entrance, or beer garden perhaps?"

"That's optimistic. If the rear resembles anything like the gothic castle the front does, I don't fancy our chances."

Gratified his partner had experienced the same reaction to the premises, Hamilton nodded in acknowledgment, and trudged on through the dank passageway.

"For a pub that's been closed for years, it still reeks of stale beer and piss down here," Clarke stuttered through coughs.

"It's a smell that never leaves." He stopped to kick an empty sleeping bag. "Or, perhaps the patrons do still come here at night."

"It's flipping eerie."

Hamilton reached out and twisted the metal handle on the old, wooden door. The rust grated in his hand as it turned and, after a few knocks with his shoulder, it squealed open to reveal a disused tip of a back garden.

"Maybe luck is on our side today," he whispered, and placed his index finger over his lips.

Clarke gave him the thumbs up before slowly pushing the door back in place. They manoeuvred around broken chairs, wooden bench tables, black bags and rolled-up stained carpets. Hamilton pictured a deserted bar inside, the place gutted and the junk left outside to rot. The two lower windows were covered with a rusty, metal mesh that couldn't be tackled quietly. The furthest window was opened ajar, and Hamilton beckoned his partner over, winking at their continued run of fortune. Clarke frowned, and lowered his ear to the opening for a few minutes.

"Someone's in there," Clarke mouthed, and Hamilton placed his face closer to his partner's, listening intently.

"What is that?" he uttered in reply.

They stepped away from the window. "That's Fifa football you're listening to, gov."

Hamilton frowned. "How do you know? Sounded like two men having a conversation."

"Two commentators, perhaps. I'm a thirty-two-year-old bachelor, I'm not mistaken, gov. And I'm pretty sure the person playing the game isn't the man who uses the sleeping bag out there. Listen again, you'll hear the faint mumble of a child's voice."

Trusting his partner, Hamilton's body sprang into action. He prized the back door open again and stood in the alleyway to contact Fraser. He needed to know how long they had to wait for the back-up team.

"They're on their way, boss, but there's been an accident on the A11 near Whitechapel High Street, and the area is gridlocked at the moment. Shall I request a patrol from the local nick?"

"Yes, do that immediately. We haven't confirmed who's in that building yet, but we have enough reason to believe it's Frankie Royal."

Hamilton re-entered the junk-filled garden and examined the back entrance. The door was firmly locked and each window shrouded in darkness. He pressed his nose against the mesh and cupped his hands between his face and the glass, desperate to find a slither of light. Thick, dark material hung behind it, restricting his view and leaving Hamilton blind to what lay on the other side. Clarke shifted slightly, remaining crouched by the crack in the window, listening for further sounds to reveal its occupants.

The vibrating phone in Hamilton's pocket startled him, and he cursed inwardly as he read Rocky's text message. Aggravated that Katy Royal had given his young officer the slip, he began searching the garden for something useful to assist in his plan. The desire to gain entry of the building, to save the missing boy and finally come face to face with the villain, burned every muscle in Hamilton's body.

CHAPTER THIRTY-SEVEN

The racket playing from the teenager's mobile phone echoed along the street, but the music did nothing to penetrate Katy's thoughts. She was oblivious to her surroundings now that she'd managed to escape the policeman's tail, and was stood in front of the pub she'd been summoned to. She had contemplated reaching out to him on the train and begging for help but, fearing for her son's life, she remained quiet and lost him as soon as possible.

Standing under The Swan's weather-beaten sign, fragments of memories from her darker days assailed her brain. Frankie's innocent face broke through the images like a beam of hope and Katy knew she had to go on. She pulled her hand from her coat pocket and examined the crumbled piece of paper, the thing she hadn't released since being rescued from the fire. The scribbled handwriting pierced her heart every time she reread it:

You want your son? I have him. This afternoon, come to the place it all began and I'll be waiting. Tell anyone... bring anyone... and your son dies. Be prepared to make a decision, Katy! P x

She drew in a lungful of air, pulled her shoulders back and reached for the brass door handle. It opened with ease and her stomach flipped as she stepped forward. All she could hope was that the monster was waiting for her and Frankie was safe.

Katy squinted, her eyes adjusting from the blue, crisp skies to the dimly-lit room. She stopped, startled by the view in front of her. The large area had been stripped of its bar, tables, stools and optics, and replaced by a sofa, coffee table and shelving unit. Exact replicas of those in her marital home.

A dark figure slithered behind her. The jingling of keys broke the stale silence. Katy turned and faced the door she'd just entered to find Pete frantically barricading them in. With the door locked, he slunk past her without a word and sat on the sofa. The football commentary droned in her ears, and she held her breath as she scanned the room for Frankie. Cautiously, she followed the path Pete had taken until she stood directly adjacent to him.

Katy gasped. "Oh my! Frankie… honey!"

"Mummy!" her son shouted, dropping the game controller to the floor.

Pete casually raised his leg, rested his foot on the table and created a barrier between mother and son. He placed one hand on the boy's knee and the other on the armrest. Katy quickly saw the shiny blade under the brute's fingers and decided against moving further. She held her hand out to Frankie, hoping he'd do the same. Pete snatched up the knife and flicked it, motioning for Katy to take the seat opposite. Tears filled her son's eyes as she listened to the silent instruction, and eased herself into the familiar wingback chair.

"Do you like what I've done with the place, Katy?" Pete sneered. "I spent a long time researching and buying your favourite things. I wanted it to look perfect, just how you like it."

"So, you were in my house before yesterday?"

Pete grinned. "Of course, many times. But don't worry I was never seen. It's just… I wanted to make this place feel homely for you… show you that I care. It's the same upstairs in the bedrooms."

His hand gripped the knife tighter. The whites of his knuckles protruded through the dried blood and scratches, as he slid himself forward to the edge of the sofa. He stared at Katy, his teeth clenched as he continued speaking.

"When I'd finally finished, and knew this place was ready for you to call home, I came to collect you. Six months ago. But you'd gone… just disappeared without a note for me, or anything. You left me."

Despite washing his face and changing his clothes, Pete was evidently in pain from his injuries. Blood seeped through his bruised and wounded skin. Katy couldn't take her eyes from his as she thought of the night she'd fled from Brad. The despair she'd felt in leaving their family home may have saved her life.

"How did you get in?" she asked.

"It always amazes me how people rush around, taking nothing in. They hop in and out of taxis all day, most of the time with bags of shopping, or a pushchair, or a screaming toddler… It's easy to drop your belongings, and I'm always there to help… although I'm never really noticed, am I? It only took a few seconds to take a photo of your set of keys before handing them back to you. You really should be more careful with the things that matter the most to you." Pete squeezed Frankie's knee harder, causing the boy's cries to escalate.

"Why didn't you just talk to me? Tell me we'd met before…"

"You would have rejected me like before…" Pete spat about betrayal and unfairness, but Katy's concentration was elsewhere.

She nodded her head occasionally, to imply she was remorseful and listening to the monster, but really her eyes focused on her son. Pete's hand slipped away and she noticed no wires, or ropes restricted Frankie further. The fear resonated off her son's face, his wobbling chin encouraged a downpour of tears, but his stillness displayed his bravery. She gave him a quick wink before returning her gaze to Pete. He had stopped speaking and his dark eyes bore into hers.

"Sorry… I –"

"Don't mug me off!" he interrupted, and launched onto his feet. "You've ruined everything and you have to pay. This could have been our home…"

"Mummy, can we go now?" Frankie whimpered, and Katy reached her hand out to him.

Pete's arm flew out, knocking her back. His momentum continued, crashing his fist into Frankie's face. Blood gushed from the boy's nose and he fell back onto the sofa, his piercing cry sounding off the wall.

Katy jumped to her feet, both hands raised in surrender. "Pete! Pete, please look at me. Don't hurt Frankie, it's me you want. I'm here."

He spun around and stepped forward until they were inches apart. His head shook, almost involuntarily, as dried saliva took root in the corners of his mouth.

"I wanted you," he breathed over Katy's face. "You fucked it up, and left me like every other woman in my life."

"You said I had a decision to make… in your note, that's what you wrote. Well, I'm here. I choose you. I've decided to be with you. I want to be with you. Just let Frankie go and we can finally be together. The two of us."

Pete frowned and stood straight. "Yes, we will be together. In death."

He reached for the silver zippo lighter on the coffee table and Frankie's sobs filled the silence of Pete's movement. He sighed heavily; rubbing his eyes with the back of his hand, the tip of the blade grazing against his skin. Katy contemplated jumping forward and knocking it from his hand, when she noticed the tanks of petrol stacked in the corner of the room next to her son. Pete's thumb repeatedly flicked the flint wheel. A scratching sound replaced by a flame, the flame replaced by the scratching sound. He toyed with her, and his plan became clear as he walked further into the room and hovered over the petrol.

Frankie raced to her side. He wrapped his small arms around her leg and she pulled his head closer into her, shielding him from the sight in front of them. Katy struggled for air, attempting to create a plan. The doors were locked. She was helpless. Her son's body trembled together with her own and she screamed.

"Stop! You can't do this. You can't kill us… Frankie is your son!"

CHAPTER THIRTY-EIGHT

"Jesus Christ! He's going to burn them alive," Hamilton cried. "I want you to get back outside and clear the vicinity while I try and talk him down."

"No way am I leaving you, gov," Clarke replied, and updated Fraser on the situation in a hushed tone over the radio.

"Fine. Find another entrance into that room while I distract him. See if you can come in from behind and surprise him."

Clarke hurried off, leaving Hamilton to plan his advance. Surprised by Katy Royal's confession, he decided there was no time to linger and sprinted back to the now broken rear door. Hamilton grabbed the metal pole they'd used to gain entry and tucked it inside his trouser waistband. He needed to be prepared for any scenario, and confronting Pete Campbell head-on may not be the wisest of decisions.

Hamilton stepped out of the side office and walked out into the main bar. It resembled a studio flat more than an old London boozer. Hamilton recognised the interior decoration immediately and anger soared through his body at the thought of such a monster intruding and violating the family's safe haven.

"Pete Campbell," Hamilton called out, and edged closer to the hostage situation. "I'm Detective Inspector Hamilton. Put your weapon down."

The bloodstained suspect remained calm and looked at Hamilton square on. Over the years, he'd realised that sometimes in life people were just pure evil. As though it were a real entity, it oozed from their pores and radiated from the darkness in their eyes. Looking at Campbell, he witnessed the full state of wretched wickedness before him, and feared there could be no positive outcome.

"We know about the other families," Hamilton said. "It's time to give it up. Nothing good will come of this."

Pete tilted his head, as if he were contemplating Hamilton's words. A sinister smile spread across the man's face, flipping the lighter up and catching it, humming all the while.

"That's interesting… *Detective Inspector Hamilton*," he sneered. "You seem to be all alone. So actually, I think a lot of good could come from this." The man pulled his thumb over the flint wheel and stared at the blue and orange flame, his fingers tapping the knife blade in his other hand.

Hamilton lurched forward, but it was too late. Clarke jumped out from behind a large pillar and onto Pete's back, striking him to the floor. Screams filled the room. The two men wrestled and Hamilton stamped furiously on the lighter, extinguishing the flame before it caught fire. He turned to find Katy Royal and her son huddled together on the floor by the sofa. Content they were safe, he moved across the room to help his partner, but was instantly met by Pete's fist. As Hamilton fell to the floor, so did the hidden metal pole, and the brute fumbled with a bunch of keys as he blundered towards the main entrance.

"Go!" Clarke groaned from the floor.

Hamilton sat up and hesitated, his attention faltering between the two men. Clarke moaned again and his head flopped back. Hamilton rushed over to find blood seeping from between his partner's fingers as he clutched his stomach.

"You've been stabbed!"

"No shit! Gov, go after him… I'll be fine."

Hamilton removed his jacket and placed it under Clarke's hand, who grunted as the blood flowed. He yelled for Katy to take over and instructed how she should place as much pressure on the wound as possible.

Clarke coughed. "Get that bastard!"

"I'll get someone in here for you!" Hamilton shouted, and ran out the door.

The entrance had been cordoned off, and two uniformed officers attempted to use themselves and their patrol car as a barrier. Civilians pushed each other and strained their necks to see what new commotion was taking place in their neighbourhood. Hamilton scanned the crowd, but couldn't get a fix on Pete Campbell or Fraser.

"Where's my officer?" he yelled to the nearest policeman.

"She headed north in pursuit of the suspect, sir, towards the station. We've requested additional back-up for her. What do you want us to do?"

"Call an ambulance immediately, we have an officer down in there."

"We have one standing by, sir. I'll move the paramedics in."

Hamilton charged along the road, as irritated bystanders yelled profanities in the wake of his chase. A swarm of people had assembled near the entrance of the train station and he sped up, worried that another member of his team had been attacked. He pushed through the masses, hollering for them to clear his path, and found an elderly woman passed out on the ground.

"Some degenerate knocked her down and she whacked her head... he didn't even bloody stop," a voice said from behind.

"Which way did he go?" Hamilton asked.

She eyed his stab vest. "Finally, a copper's on scene. We need some medical assistance for this –"

"Madam, which way did he go?"

The woman rolled her eyes and pointed away from the train station. "Ran down that alley."

"Thank you. Can you ensure an ambulance has been called?" he said, and took flight once again, before the woman could challenge him.

A chaotic buzz occupied the high street as the mid-afternoon pursuit propelled the locals' curiosity. Hamilton ran out into the road, ignoring the protesting car horns as he dashed across. Leaping and swerving the oncoming traffic and then the pedestrians, he headed through the backstreets. He peered along the residential street the alley had brought him on to, and spied a figure entering a gate to a small playground at the end of the road. Hamilton scurried to the right, landing in the bushes, obscuring the wooden perimeter of the play area. He searched for a loose panel, kicking each board until one swung against the next. *You can always rely on local kids wanting a secret meet-up after hours.*

Hamilton crouched and angled his body, one leg and then his head peering through the slats. He pulled himself free and slipped behind a large oak tree, the long branches shadowing his presence. Pete Campbell strolled closer on the pathway, the knife clutched in his fist, his head scanning from side-to-side and over his shoulder. Hamilton's eyes searched a route. One wrong move and he'd be stabbed as easily as his partner.

Pete's attention fell on a group of children skirting around the slide. Hamilton took the opportunity and leapt out from his hiding place behind the suspect, tackling him to the ground. His unexpected attack caused the blade to catapult from Pete's hand as the man's head smacked down hard onto the gravelled path.

"Sir, you okay?"

Hamilton smiled at the familiar voice as he reached for his handcuffs. Rocky knelt down beside him, but the assistance was unnecessary; Peter Campbell was unconscious.

"I'm fine, lad."

"I exited the train station, sir, and saw you racing across the road. I shouted your name…"

"Call this in for me, Rocky. I need to find Fraser. She was tracking the suspect, but I haven't seen her."

Hamilton reached for his mobile phone, fingers heavily stained with his partner's blood, and hit the third speed dial button. A groggy voice mumbled an answer after three rings.

"Fraser! Where are you?"

"Boss... I lost him."

"We've got him. Are you okay?"

She groaned. "Yeah… I'm fine. I'm on the high street."

"Get yourself back to The Swan and check in on Clarke. If the ambulance hasn't already left, I want you to go with him and keep me updated at all times."

"But, boss... what about Campbell?"

Hamilton detected a strain in her voice, and wondered if the suspect had dented her pride by escaping, or if she was holding something back from him. Distant sirens grew closer to the playground and Pete yelped, struggling as Rocky dragged the man to his feet.

"Something you need to tell me, Fraser?"

She hesitated. "No. I just don't want him to take flight again, boss."

"Don't worry... there's no chance of that. Now, please get back to Clarke, I'll join you at the hospital as soon as I can."

CHAPTER THIRTY-NINE

Hamilton knocked on the door and entered the private hospital room. He was surprised to find the bed empty and walked further inside. The door to the en-suite bathroom opened and Katy Royal stepped out and shrugged.

"Never had such treatment in hospital before. No private rooms for me, not even when I gave birth to Frankie."

He smiled, and sat in the visitor's chair while Katy perched on the bed, her feet dangling and grazing along the floor. She was still fully dressed, the hospital gown abandoned beside her.

"I won't keep you," Hamilton said. "I just wanted to check on you and your son."

"They're examining my injuries from yesterday… gosh, I can't believe what's happened in such a short space of time. Anyway, I'm fine. It's Frankie I'm worried about. He seems unharmed, but they've got a few experts confirming that and he's with a counsellor at the moment."

"That's good to hear."

"How's your partner?"

"He's going to be just fine. There'll be a nice scar, but the wound wasn't fatal. He's currently enjoying all the attention he's receiving," Hamilton chuckled.

"Thank you… to you both. You saved our lives."

"That's our job." Hamilton stood up to leave and Katy bowed her head. A sense of sadness filled him. "Can I ask you a question?"

"Yes, of course."

"Is Pete Campbell really Frankie's father, or was that a lie to save you both?"

Katy sighed and wiped a single tear from her cheek. "I wish I knew for sure, Inspector. All this time I thought Brad had saved me from a life filled with depression and sadness. When my parents died, I couldn't face the pain. I sailed through denial and did whatever I could to keep me from the truth… that I would never see them again. I took Brad's possessiveness for concern, and when I discovered I was pregnant just a few weeks into the relationship, it was as though I'd been given a second chance. I could have a family again and rectify my life."

"So, the connection with Campbell was?"

"I didn't know it was Pete… I still don't fully recall all the things he said. When Frankie was born, I was confused with the dates and realised things didn't totally add up." Katy looked away from Hamilton. "I'm ashamed to say, I brushed the thoughts away, thinking and hoping my son was premature. I know I've made some bad choices in my life, but I'm not a slapper, Inspector. When Pete mentioned us meeting five years ago, it would have been just before I met Brad… I honestly can't remember."

Hamilton bridged the gap and touched Katy's shoulder. She finally looked up at him, her blue eyes glazed with tears. He could see the past haunted her, it was a feeling he understood, and he hoped she could somehow find peace.

"Katy, it's human nature to make mistakes. What proves your character is how you learn from them, how you move on, and how you turn your life around."

"Frankie… what if that monster is… I mean, what if my son grows up to be like Pete?" She grunted. "Or like Brad?"

He rested on the bed next to the heartbroken woman. "I do not believe the craving to hurt and damage another human being is innate. It's how we live, our society and the people we look to for guidance and support that help shape who we are. Plus, you don't even know if Campbell is your son's father. You've admitted where you've gone wrong, but you still have a chance to do something about it. Counselling may also be a good place for you to start."

"I've just run away from everything for so long."

"Well, stop running. Show Frankie there are more ways to deal with your pain. Everything you've done has been for your son, so I have faith you can turn this around and create a positive future for both of you. No matter how they come to us, every child is a blessing, Katy... treasure your son," Hamilton said.

He patted Katy's hand and she smiled a smile he'd seen before – the unspoken thank you. A knock at the door finalised their conversation and Hamilton stood up as Matthew and Alexina entered the room. He bid them farewell, and explained they would all need to visit the station to make official statements.

The atmosphere changed in the room. The chatter increased and Hamilton couldn't help but peer over his shoulder before leaving. He glimpsed a change in Katy instantly. There was a determination and willpower in her animated gestures as she spoke to her friends. They hung on her every word, flooded with concern and interest. Hamilton walked away, content that no matter the outcome of any paternity test, Katy Royal would use her new, genuine relationships to finally build a safe home for her and her innocent child.

Fraser and Rocky were still with Clarke when he returned to his partner's bedside. He congratulated them on a successful arrest.

"When will you interview him, gov?" Clarke asked.

Hamilton glanced at his watch. "Tomorrow morning. Pete Campbell is safe in custody and we haven't been home in over twenty-four hours. I don't want to make any mistakes with him, so the three of us will reconvene in the incident room first thing and collect our information. Fraser, do you want to do the interview with me?"

When she didn't answer, Rocky jabbed her in the ribs. "Sorry, boss. What was that?"

"Campbell's interview?"

"Oh! Yes, I'd like to be there with you, boss."

Hamilton instructed his team to go home and rest, and reminded Clarke to be on his best behaviour. His partner laughed off the remark. He was grateful luck had stayed on their side; if Campbell's knife attack had penetrated Clarke's stomach any deeper, the result would have been fatal. After bidding their colleague farewell, leaving just Rocky to make his own way home, Hamilton was finally alone with Fraser. They took the stairs, strolling towards the exit.

"What happened out there today when you were pursuing Campbell?"

She shrugged. "It's all still hazy, boss… but, I think I was punched from behind."

"By him?"

"I assumed so, but now I'm not too sure. I stopped briefly to check someone stayed with the elderly woman he'd knocked down, then I thought I saw him escape in the opposite direction and I ran like hell after him… except, where you arrested him was in the opposite direction. I just don't think he could have backtracked, whacked me over the head and made it to the park before you."

"Are you in pain?"

Fraser rubbed the back of her head. "No. I went down like a sack of spuds, but I think it was more shock… and shame," she said, holding up her grazed palms and wrists.

Hamilton stopped. "Do you need to get checked out?"

"Don't be silly, boss. I fell over like a kid in a playground. A nice, hot bath will take care of all this."

As they approached the car park, Hamilton remembered Fraser had arrived in the ambulance with Clarke, and therefore her car was still in Stratford. He offered to drive her back to collect it.

"I'll call an Uber, boss. Get home before your wife divorces you."

"She'd divorce me if she found out I'd let a young woman get in one of those taxis alone at night."

Fraser laughed. "Slightly sexist, but I get your point. I'd better accept then, thank you."

During the short drive, Hamilton suggested they request any CCTV footage from Stratford High Street, as a way of determining who had attacked Fraser.

"I really don't think there's much point, boss. The place was swarming with people. It was probably one of those youngsters, who hate the police and thought they'd help their brother-in-arms escape."

Hamilton grunted. "You could have a point there. But, I'll get Rocky to look into it all the same."

"He's been a helpful addition to the team."

"Definite potential there I think. Which reminds me, I must touch base with Wedlock before calling it a night."

"It's awful what's happened to his mum… If he does have to look after her full-time, it will be a difficult job for him to do alone. Pass my best wishes onto him please, boss."

A comfortable silence filled the car, and Fraser stared out the window until they arrived at the spot they'd parked a few hours earlier. The crime scene ribbon around the front entrance of the Swan fluttered in the breeze, the night only adding to the dark atmosphere of the street.

Fraser got out of the vehicle and lowered her head back into the car. "Boss, ever get the feeling you're being watched?"

He looked at his colleague and smiled. "In this job, Fraser, always."

CHAPTER FORTY

At the beginning of the interview, Hamilton stated Pete Campbell's refusal for legal representation for the benefit of the tape. Once again, he glared into the murderer's soulless eyes and, despite having washed away the mask of bloodstains, the man's various abrasions were a painful reminder of the heinous crimes he'd committed. With the monster in custody, jubilation soared through Hamilton's body.

"Pete Campbell, you have been arrested for the attempted murder of Katy and Frankie Royal and Matthew Webb. In light of securing your DNA, we're confident charges will also be brought forward for the murders of Emma and Kyle Jones and Scarlett and Noah Mitchell –"

"Nooo. Nooo." Campbell's unnerving tone haunted the small interview room.

"Mr Campbell, you left this note for Katy Royal in her London apartment, is that correct?"

Hamilton slid the transparent wallet across the table and identified its evidence number. Campbell didn't flinch.

"I'm now showing the suspect another sheet of paper which was found at his place of residence," Hamilton continued, and inwardly cheered when the man's eyes flickered down to the table for a moment. "We found this in the shed in your garden. Although, it's more like a criminal workstation than a mere garden shed. Isn't that right, Mr Campbell?"

"I wouldn't know. I rent it out to someone… a neighbour."

Hamilton folded his arms over his chest. "Really? Can you supply us with this someone's name? No? Could you explain why this paper, and the book accompanying it, are written in the same handwriting as Katy Royal's note? Why your finger prints are all over it, and why it was found in *your* shed? This book is a diary of events, detailing daily activities of all three female victims – going back as far as two years in Katy's case." He sat forward and thumbed through the pages. "Frequent taxi pick-up and drop-off locations, routine shopping trips and other personal information. You managed to get close to these women and yet stay invisible. They felt safe around you."

Campbell smirked, and relaxed back into the chair. Continuing to stare only at Hamilton, the man listened to every question and comment, but remained verbally unresponsive.

"And the work you did with those keys." Hamilton changed track and leisurely applauded. "I honestly had no idea it was so simple to copy a key… photograph the original, print and cut the template to fit the blank one, a bit of drilling and hey presto!"

The suspect sneered, nodding his head at the appreciation he was receiving. Hamilton slammed his fist on the table and jumped up from his seat.

"It sickens me to know you've used what was innocent sharing of information on YouTube, and twisted it to your vile crimes. To intrude and stalk and take the lives of innocent people!"

Hamilton's spittle landed on the desk. The pair exchanged scowls, neither one ready to back down, until Fraser cleared her throat and dragged Hamilton from the image of violated corpses. He sat down and collected his emotions.

"We know all about your ex-girlfriend, Rita, Mr Campbell." Hamilton paused, and enjoyed the look of fear now shadowing the man's face. "Oh yes, we found her and explained everything. Rita's travelling back to London as we speak, with the intention of testifying against you."

Before the interview, and in light of Campbell's arrest, Hamilton had managed to persuade Rita's protective mother to share her daughter's contact details. He heard the relief in Rita's voice as he clarified the recent circumstances and that there was little chance of Campbell's freedom. Rita explained her ex's obsessive nature and how, once he had a plan set in his sights, nothing would stop him. Pete's need to control and know everything had pushed her into running away. Her statement, coupled with the information that Campbell's mother had died when he was an unstable five-year-old, had gone some way to explaining Campbell's neurotic character. The man's need to attach himself and dominate the women in his life had only escalated when he met Katy Royal. His violent behaviour triggered to breaking point when she became the true object of affection test he couldn't have.

"As well as your DNA over the equipment in your *work* shed, tests are currently in process to determine if it matches the samples taken from your second victim." Images of the women and children's faces disturbed Hamilton's thoughts again. "There are some vile creatures in prison, Mr Campbell… but even they don't condone child killers. You'll be lower than scum in there, and I'll do my utmost to ensure the serving jury give you the maximum sentence for your crimes."

Rage simmered beneath the surface, and Hamilton could feel the imminent eruption inside him. Sometimes, it wasn't enough to arrest the monsters. Just sometimes he wanted to be left alone in a room with the murderers of this world. He wasn't one to tolerate unnecessary violence, but Campbell's unremorseful demeanour, combined with the memory of those children, caused Hamilton to clench and unclench his fists repeatedly.

The interview felt pointless. Campbell wasn't sharing anything new and they had all the physical evidence they needed. Yet, Hamilton remained unsatisfied.

"Just tell us why, Campbell. Why did you kill those mothers and sons in their home?"

"Why, why, why… That's all anyone ever asks," Campbell finally retorted.

"What should I be asking?"

The man's fingers drummed on top of the table. "Listen to me… Katy is mine! She always will be, wherever she goes. I was furious when she left me. Just like Rita before her and…"

"Your mother before that?" Hamilton finished the sentence.

Campbell's nostrils flared, his cheeks flushed a deep red.

"Except your mother died. There was no choice for her. What you did… you made a decision to end those women's lives, didn't you? So, my question remains, Mr Campbell, why?"

The monster in front of him parted his lips and slowly sucked in a mouthful of air. Glowering at Hamilton, Campbell shrugged and finally answered, "Because I could."

The interview door opened and the desk sergeant slipped a note to Hamilton before exiting just as swiftly as he'd entered. He read it and passed it to Fraser who, until this point, had purely observed.

"We've just had some good news from the lab, Mr Campbell," she said. "Your DNA is an exact match to the pubic hair retrieved from Scarlett Mitchell's mouth. Plus, the makeshift keys recovered from your shed opened all the front doors of the victims' homes. We're also investigating the attack and attempted murder of Brad Royal, and your involvement in it. You will be charged and sent to trial for each and every crime."

Hamilton waited for a response from Campbell, who simply stared ahead and ignored Fraser while she spoke. There wasn't a shred of remorse from the man, and Hamilton felt a pinch of disappointment. He wanted to understand why those women and children had lost their lives. He wanted to know the exact moment and reasoning of Campbell's decisions to snatch away any future they'd had. But, Hamilton knew today would not be the day his questions were answered, if in fact he would ever find a resolution for them. As much as he tried, sometimes, there was no way to get inside the mind of a killer. Instead, Hamilton chose to celebrate the success of his team, saving a third mother and son from a fatal encounter, and extracting another villain from the streets of London.

EPILOGUE

Hamilton opened the door to the last of his guests. The woman's tanned skin glistened in the sunshine, and her hourglass figure hugged the white linen dress stopping just above her knee. Although her beauty was undeniable, he couldn't help but detect a sternness in her expression as her brown eyes darted around the hallway. Hamilton smiled and welcomed her through, hoping for more of a relaxed atmosphere today. The corners of her mouth turned up, exposing a single dimple in her left cheek, and she silently followed him through his home and out into the garden.

It wasn't an enormous space, most central London houses don't offer that luxury, but it was a sanctuary for him and his wife. Elizabeth was the green-fingered one of the pair, and had spent a lot of time tending to the area since their daughter died, even planting a small primrose tree in Maggie's memory. He smelt the sweet scent from the yellow heart-shaped leaves as he stepped onto the patio. It was weird and wonderful to see the place so busy with life.

"Everyone, can I just ask you all to stop chatting for a moment?" he called out. "I'd like to unofficially introduce Detective Sergeant Yasmine Dixon. And, although today isn't about work, or investigations, or anything formal, I thought it would be a nice opportunity to get us all together."

"First time I've been invited around to the big man's house, and I've been his partner for four years." Clarke laughed, and accepted another can of beer from Elizabeth.

"And it will be the last if you ever call me big man again – injured or not," Hamilton retorted with a wink. "Anyway, as I was

Epilogue

saying... we've got ourselves a new team here and I thought that needed celebrating."

Hamilton had taken some time the previous evening to speak with his colleague, Les Wedlock, who had requested a transfer to the Kent Constabulary after his mother's failing health. Though saddened to lose an experienced member of the team, Hamilton empathised with his family values. He decided to take a punt, and offered a place on his team to an officer desperate to climb the ranks. After discussing the matter with DCI Allen, Rocky had been offered a promotion. He knew it was a big step for the lad, but having observed how he worked the last case, Hamilton saw great potential in the new recruit.

"Before I let Dixon... sorry, Yasmine, get a word in, I would just like to congratulate DC O'Connor. Although I'm sure it'll be difficult to call you anything else but Rocky, now that name has certainly stuck in my head."

"To Rocky!" they called in unison, and raised their glasses.

Yasmine brushed the long strands of black hair from her face and smiled. "I'll admit, this is quite intimidating... My public speaking is usually confined to an office or crime scene. I'm sure I'll talk to you all individually at some point today, so for now I'd just like to apologise to you all. I know you were expecting me sooner, especially to help out on the last investigation, but I couldn't leave my last case without seeing it through to the end."

"That's something we can all understand," Clarke chimed in.

Hamilton stepped away to add more coal to the BBQ fire, while Elizabeth turned up the music.

"That's enough office banter," she said, and gave Hamilton a kiss on the cheek before re-joining Yasmine. "So, love, tell us more about you."

"Well, I've been married to my husband, Warren, for ten years and we have two beautiful children, Sabrina and Ali. I was born in Marrakesh, but have lived in London since I was two."

"Oh, I've always wanted to visit Morocco," Elizabeth said. "That word, Marrakesh... I just love how it rolls off the tongue."

Epilogue

Hamilton frowned as he stood near the primrose tree. "You okay?" he asked Fraser. "Looking a bit distracted today."

"It's nothing, boss."

"Hey! For today, it's Denis."

She smiled, but there was no sign of any happiness in her eyes. He probed her further for an answer.

"Well, my cat hasn't come home."

Hamilton raised his eyebrows and nodded, unsure how to reply.

"Sorry, this isn't the time to talk cats," she said, and turned to rejoin the group.

"Listen, I don't have a pet, and I'm more of a dog person anyway, but I do know that people who have them, see them as family."

"Exactly! I've had Felix for three years, and he's never stayed away from home this long."

Hamilton shrugged. "Perhaps, working on the Campbell case, and you not being home as often meant the cat couldn't get in, or a neighbour fed him and so he's prowling about having a good time. It's something like that, I bet you."

"Yes, I'm sure you're right, and I must sound so pathetic. Time for another drink... *Denis.*" She laughed as she walked away, stopping next to Rocky and the cooler box of drinks.

Hamilton returned to his command station at the BBQ, ensuring he had the necessary cooking utensils ready. He watched the women laugh together, Clarke chilling on the sun lounger, and listened to the chatter and noise as it drifted through the air. An uncharacteristically warm feeling washed over him, and he smiled. While it was strange to have work colleagues in his garden, to see his wife interact with members of the MIT – people he'd steered her away from in fear of reviving painful emotions – it was uplifting to have finally invited these colleagues, and friends, into his home.

THE END

ACKNOWLEDGEMENTS

I'd like to take this opportunity to thank my family and close friends. Without them, No Safe Home would simply be an idea in the pages of my notebook. Your constant faith is inspiring.

A special shout out to the readers. You all continually amaze me with your enthusiasm, and all you do for the love of books. For the endless support and promotion, huge thanks to the #BlogSquad, The Haphazardous Hippo, Bookstormer, The Great British Book Off, Emma the Book Worm, My Chestnut Reading Tree, Linda's Book Bag, Damp Pebbles and The Writing Garnet. To the amazing people at Book Connectors, Crime Book Club, UK Crime Book Club, Crime Fiction Addicts and to every member of The Book Club (I hope you enjoy this in your pants).

Finally, to the formidable Bloodhound Books team and author gang – a massive thank you for your support, encouragement, expert opinions and friendships, all of which made DI Hamilton's return possible.